SUNLIGHT ON THE ROCKS

A Comedy in Two Acts

by Theresa Rebeck

A SAMUEL FRENCH ACTING EDITION

SAMUEL FRENCH
FOUNDED 1830

SAMUELFRENCH.COM

ISBN 978-0-573-69553-7   Printed in U.S.A.   #21828

MUSIC USE NOTE

Licensees are solely responsible for obtaining formal written permission from copyright owners to use copyrighted music in the performance of this play and are strongly cautioned to do so. If no such permission is obtained by the licensee, then the licensee must use only original music that the licensee owns and controls. Licensees are solely responsible and liable for all music clearances and shall indemnify the copyright owners of the play and their licensing agent, Samuel French, Inc., against any costs, expenses, losses and liabilities arising from the use of music by licensees.

IMPORTANT BILLING AND CREDIT REQUIREMENTS

All producers of *SUNDAY ON THE ROCKS* *must* give credit to the Author of the Play in all programs distributed in connection with performances of the Play, and in all instances in which the title of the Play appears for the purposes of advertising, publicizing or otherwise exploiting the Play and/or a production. The name of the Author *must* appear on a separate line on which no other name appears, immediately following the title and *must* appear in size of type not less than fifty percent of the size of the title type.

Premier production at LONG WHARF THEATRE
May 3, 1994

SUNDAY
ON THE ROCKS

by THERESA REBECK

directed by
SUSANN BRINKLEY

Unit set design by
HUGH LANDWEHR

production stage manager
C.A. CLARK

CAST (in order of appearance)

Elly	KRISTIN FLANDERS
Gayle	JENNIFER VAN DYCK
Jen	MIA KORF
Jessica	PATRICIA CORNELL

Set Coordination and Properties: David Fletcher
Costume Coordination: Patricia M. Risser
Lighting: Kirk Matson
Sound Brenton Evans
Script Development; Sari Bodi
Artistic Director: Arvin Brown
Executive Director: M. Edgar Rosenblum

CHARACTERS

ELLY - A talkative, excitable woman, 30 years old.

GAYLE - A woman of few words, intelligent and wry, 34.

JEN - A loose, casual, very likable woman, 29.

JESSICA - A slight, pretty, seemingly gentle woman with a will of iron, 30. On the surface, she looks very much like any of the others--it is important not to distinguish her from them in terms of costume.

NOTE:
1. There is nothing self-pitying about these women. Although their conversation chronicles their past mistakes, they are good humored about it all. The first act should be played lightly, almost like a comedy. There is nothing vicious about their laughter.

2. The description of Elly's mother on page 55 should be tailored to resemble the actress who plays Jessica.

SET

The back porch of a slightly weather-beaten house, not necessarily screened in. There is a small table set stage right, and the door to the house at the opposite end of the porch. Three wicker chairs are scattered about the porch. The door leads to a comfortable, quite tidy living room with a small couch, an easy chair, a floor lamp and stereo. Elly's purse and a couple of books have been set on the couch. A door to the left of the living room leads to the kitchen and the bedrooms upstairs. It is a beautiful Sunday morning in the early autumn. The day promises to be quite warm.

ACT I

Scene 1
Breakfast on the Back Porch

(The lights come up on ELLY, who sits on the porch, holding a large glass of scotch over ice. She takes a drink and shudders. GAYLE enters from the house, carrying breakfast fixings and a half-empty glass of orange juice.)

GAYLE. *(She notices the scotch.)* What are you doing?

ELLY. I'm drinking scotch.

GAYLE. You're drinking scotch.

ELLY. Yes, I'm drinking scotch.

GAYLE. El, it's nine thirty in the morning.

ELLY. I know, I'm having it for breakfast. Like F. Scott Fitzgerald. I read that about him, I think, he was such an incredible alcoholic he would have, like, scotch for breakfast.

GAYLE. Yeah, but you're not an alcoholic

ELLY. Wait a minute. It might have been Hemingway. Was Hemingway an alcoholic?

GAYLE. I don't know, but—

ELLY. Maybe it was Dorothy Parker. It doesn't matter. A lot of writers were alcoholics, and I'm sure one of them drank scotch for breakfast.

GAYLE. But you're not a writer. You're in advertising.

ELLY. Other people do it, too. When I was in college, I knew all these guys who would go one binges and drink all weekend, non-stop. I'm not kidding. Also--ALSO, have you

ever gone to one of those fancy Sunday brunches they have at
these fabulous hotels? Waiters wander around the room with
these bottles of champagne, you know, and everyone gets
bombed at 11 in the morning. OR many people won't drink
the champagne because it doesn't have enough kick, so to
speak, and so they have Bloody Marys. And this doesn't only
happen in fancy hotels, mind you; I've seen it in normal
restaurants, people getting bombed on Sunday mornings. So
this morning I am taking part in a long and honored tradition.

GAYLE. You've thought this through, haven't you?

ELLY. I've just never done it. You know, I have never had a
drink before like four in the afternoon. I've never had a drink
in the morning.

GAYLE. So why are you starting now?

ELLY. I'm pregnant.

(Pause.)

GAYLE. Oh. *(Pause.)* God, I'm sorry, El.

ELLY. Please don't be sorry. This is not something to be
sorry about; it is not something to be happy about. It's just
something that *is,* you know, something that happens to people.
Some people get pregnant; some people drink in the morning.
I really don't think there's any morality connected to the condition.

GAYLE. Oh, God. Are you going to start talking about
morality?

ELLY. Why not?

GAYLE. Then I'm going to join you.

(GAYLE takes the bottle and pours herself a drink.)

ELLY. Haven't you ever been curious about drinking in the morning?

GAYLE. I've done it.

ELLY. You have? When?

GAYLE. Give me one of your ice cubes. Many many years ago. I was very uptight at the time. God, Jessica is going to freak if she catches us.

ELLY. No, she's already gone. She went to church with Jeffrey.

GAYLE. Oh, great. She's going to come back all holy and find us getting hammered on the back porch.

ELLY. No, they were going to take a long drive in the country because it's such a lovely day. Perhaps late in the afternoon, they'll stop by a roadside inn and have tea—

GAYLE. Oh, that sounds very nice.

ELLY. Yes, they have--the perfect relationship.

(Pause.)

GAYLE. Does Roger know?

ELLY. About Jessica and Jeff and their perfect relationship?

GAYLE. Do you think you could not be coy about this?

ELLY. Yes, Roger knows. I told Roger last night, and now Roger knows.

GAYLE. What did he say?

ELLY. He said, I'm sorry. I don't know why, but whenever I tell someone I'm pregnant it brings out their need to apologize.

GAYLE. Who else have you told?

ELLY. No one. It's just that everyone at the gynecologist's

office couldn't apologize enough. And try to imagine how stupid you feel, in a gynecologist's office, saying to everyone, "Hey--it's not your fault."

GAYLE. Did Roger say anything besides 'I'm sorry?'

ELLY. Yes, he said, "What are you going to do about it?"

GAYLE. Oh.

ELLY. Look, could you stop saying "Oh" like it's the end of the world? It is not the end of the world.

GAYLE. I'm sorry. From now on, I'll say only the exactly right thing.

ELLY. I'm sorry.

GAYLE. Do you think you have enough scotch in you to talk about this yet?

ELLY. I don't know. Yes. I can talk about this. This isn't that big a deal.

GAYLE. Right. So what did Roger say?

ELLY. Roger. Roger, Roger. Roger said what are you going to do, I said I'm going to have an abortion--and--he offered to marry me.

GAYLE. He did?

ELLY. Yes, but I thought he was going to choke to death. You should have seen him strangling out the words; he was absolutely terrified that I would take him up on it. So I said, calm down, I'm not going to marry you, we don't have the money, we're not ready, etc., etc., and HE said, well, it's just that he could never bring himself to have an abortion.

GAYLE. He did.

ELLY. Yes. And I got mad.

GAYLE. You did.

ELLY. Yes. So I said, that's right, you fucking asshole, you couldn't bring yourself to have an abortion because you've never had to fucking think about it, because it's my fucking problem because it's my fucking body, and you can afford to just sit there and wash your hands of the whole damn thing because we're not talking about *your* being pregnant for nine months; we're talking about *me.*

GAYLE. What did he say to that?

ELLY. Oh, he went into this whole song and dance about how he would stick by me, la la la la la--he loves me--I told him to get lost--he told me I was flying off the handle--you know how these things go. So, at some point, I just got completely mad and left. Do you want some more scotch?

GAYLE. I have a lot.

ELLY. Have some more.

(ELLY pours more scotch into GAYLE'S glass. JEN enters from the kitchen, carrying the Sunday paper.)

JEN. Oh, God, you're out here! I've been looking all over the house for you. I thought you guys deserted me and went out to get donuts or something. God, I would love a donut. Jesus, you're drinking scotch.

ELLY. Cocktails at brunch.

GAYLE. It's an old and honored tradition.

JEN. "Cocktails at brunch" is a Bloody Mary at 11. Scotch on the rocks at 9:30 is not the same thing.

ELLY. Do you want some?

JEN. I don't know. Where's Jessica?

(JEN looks around suspiciously, pushes ELLY'S feet off the chair and stares at it.)

ELLY. Gone for the day. Off for a jaunt in the country with Jeffrey. I'll get you a glass.

JEN. You punched a hole in Jessica's chair.

ELLY. They're not Jessica's chairs. They're *our* chairs. Remember? We all paid for them. They're OUR chairs.

JEN. Yeah, I know, but they're really her chairs, you know? I mean, *I* didn't want them.

GAYLE. Me neither.

ELLY. Well, I sure didn't want them. I hate wicker. Why do we do that?

JEN. I don't know. But she's going to throw a fit when she sees this hole.

ELLY. Well, fine. If she's going to inflict wicker on us, she can just take the consequences.

(ELLY goes into the house. JEN sits down, looking at the newspaper, somewhat preoccupied.)

JEN. You know, it really is kind of ridiculous the way we let her push us around. I mean, it's not like she's our mother.

GAYLE. Jen.

JEN. I can't believe we're doing this. Can you believe this? The last time I got drunk in the morning I was in high school. Oh, God, I hope Richardson doesn't call. I mean, it's hard enough to talk to him when I'm sober. I guess he called about 14 times yesterday while I was at the mall. Jessica left all these little notes on my bed--you know those little tiny white notes she leaves everywhere? It looked like it was snowing in there.

GAYLE. Jen--Elly's pregnant.

JEN. Oh, Jesus, no kidding. Really? God. That's really too bad. But you know, she better not tell Jessica. Do you want the comics?

GAYLE. Jen!

JEN. I heard you: Elly's pregnant. I just don't think it's that big a deal. Is she going to have an abortion?

GAYLE. Yes.

JEN. Well.

GAYLE. You know, this isn't a non-event.

(ELLY reenters with a glassful of ice. She puts some in her glass, some in GAYLE'S and pours scotch for JEN. She then reveals a pack of cigarettes and deals them out.)

ELLY. I don't think it's a non-event. I never said that. Here we have cigarettes. In honor of the scotch for breakfast, I bought a pack of cigarettes today.

JEN. Oh, God, I would *love* a cigarette.

(JEN and GAYLE take cigarettes; ELLY pulls out a lighter and lights them all around. Everyone enjoys their first puff with great relish. ELLY crosses front and center and peers out toward the street.)

ELLY. With my luck, Jessica and Jeffrey will stop by after Mass to pick up sweaters or something. She'll take one look at this and kick me out. She's just looking for an excuse.

JEN. Isn't that the truth? God, she wanted to get rid of you over that stupid Campbell's soup thing. (GAYLE kicks her.) OWWWW. What did you kick me f-- Oh, Jesus, Gayle, it's not like Elly doesn't know. OOOOWWWW.

(GAYLE has kicked her again, harder.)

ELLY. What did she say to you?

GAYLE. Nothing.

ELLY. What is the point of drinking scotch in the morning if you're not going to tell the truth?

JEN. She said just the sort of shit you'd expect her to. She said you weren't fitting into the spirit of the household--you know, stuff about integrity and Christian non violent resistance to the capitalist system--I don't know. What else did she say? She doesn't like the way you wash dishes. The same stuff.

ELLY. She wanted to kick me out over a fucking can of soup?

GAYLE. You knew it was going to make her mad when you bought it. I was with you. Jesus, that was *why* you bought it, to make her mad.

ELLY. I bought it because I like mushroom soup.

GAYLE. You could've bought Purity Supreme mushroom soup.

ELLY. Purity Supreme doesn't make—

GAYLE. Yes it does—

ELLY No, it doesn't make the kind of mushroom soup that I like. I like golden mushroom soup. Purity Supreme makes cream of mushroom soup, and I don't like that kind.

GAYLE. You could have hid it in your room and had it some night when she was out. You put it in the pantry, you knew she was going to see it—

ELLY. I resent being told what I can eat and what I can't! And aside from the fact that she's the only person in America still boycotting soup, it was always a stupid boycott, I've tried to explain that to you—

JEN. Oh, no.

ELLY. There are two kinds of boycotts: Practical boycotts and ideological boycotts.

GAYLE. El—

ELLY. If it's a practical boycott, then you take part in it because you're trying to hurt the company's business. And those are *big* boycotts; you have to have a lot of people doing them or they don't work, like the Nestle boycott. The other kind, the ideological kind, you take part in because it's like your moral duty. You know you're really not making a dent, but you do it because it's the right thing to do.

JEN. I never understood this argument.

GAYLE. That's because it's a stupid argument.

ELLY It's not! The point is, nobody ever believed in the Campbells boycott, so if we're going to do it, it's only because of the ideological thing, because we, like, hate what they're doing to the farmworkers. But all the other canning companies are doing it to the farmworkers too, so we have to boycott everybody. If we boycott Campbells, we have to boycott DelMonte, and Purity Supreme and Dole--if it's a moral issue it applies across the board, doesn't it? But nobody's going to give up canned everything, even Jessica likes her little can of beets.

GAYLE. El, this argument is stupid.

ELLY. No, it's not, if you think about it—

JEN. Who wants to think about it? It's not that big a deal to boycott Campbell's soup.

ELLY. *(Yelling.)* IT IS IF YOU LIKE GOLDEN MUSHROOM!

JEN. All right! I just don't understand what the big deal is—

ELLY. *(Ranting a little.)* It's the principal of the thing! God! If Jessica had a good reason for insisting that I boycott the fucking soup, I'd do it gladly, I'd picket the company, I'd quit my job and teach English to poor little migrant children for the rest of my life! But she doesn't have a good reason! It's the same damn thing with Roger! If he had a good reason that I shouldn't have an abortion, I wouldn't! I wouldn't! But he doesn't have nay reason, he hasn't thought it through for a second. It's all just out there--boycott soup, don't have abortions, all these horrible things floating around the ozone, these *things* I'm not supposed to do because they make me a terrible person, and no one can really give me a good reason why. WHY?

GAYLE. Oh, come on, you know that's not true.

ELLY. I don't know that's not true.

GAYLE. You want reasons why? You want to know why you shouldn't have an abortion? Roger will give you reasons.

JEN. Jessica will give you reasons—

ELLY. No, they won't. They'll just go into some routine about murder or something. I mean, they just don't seem to be able to get it through their thick fucking skulls that this is not a moral issue, it's a *social* issue—

GAYLE. Jesus, El, would you listen to yourself? You don't really want reasons from people! You just want to argue! You just want to be right about everything—

ELLY. That's not true. I don't need to be right. I need to be *convinced.* If they're going to tell me I'm all fucked up and immoral, they better back up their arguments. I just think if you're going to judge somebody, you ought to be able to convince them too.

(Pause.)

GAYLE. (To JEN.) Did you follow that?

JEN. Kind of. But I just kind of think it's stupid, you know? I mean--people don't work like that. There's just always going to be somebody who thinks you're awful and there's nothing you can do about it. Can I have some more scotch?

(ELLY pushes the bottle to JEN.)

ELLY. Well, coming from you, that philosophy is not entirely surprising.

(Pause. JEN puts down the bottle.)

GAYLE. *El.*

JEN. Oh. Is that supposed to be an insult? Are you trying to insult me?

ELLY. No, I just meant—

JEN. I know what you meant. You meant I sleep around a lot.

ELLY. No, I didn't—

GAYLE. Yes you did.

ELLY. I didn't mean anything, it just came out of my mouth.

JEN. I don't care if that is what you meant. I do sleep around, I don't sleep around alot. I sleep around. I have always believed that sex is just really, really fun, and I'm not going to change my attitude now. I like sex. That doesn't mean I'm a loon about it. I don't pick up guys on streetcorners. I don't parade total strangers through the house. I mean, I'm not Wilt Chamberlain, for God's sake.

GAYLE. No one said you were.

JEN. I sleep with my friends. I don't sleep with anybody I haven't known for at least two weeks. And I'm completely careful. I take every precaution in the book. Those people who say safe sex isn't fun? They've never met me. I've never had a venereal disease, I've never been pregnant—

ELLY. All right—

JEN. It's not like I'm a prostitute.

GAYLE. All right.

JEN. Jesus, I don't even have affairs with married men! Okay, okay, *once* I had an affair with a married man. But just once.

(Pause.)

ELLY. *(Curious.)* You did?

JEN. *(Admission.)* Yeah, so what? That hardly makes me a homewrecker.

GAYLE. When?

ELLY. I know who it was. It was that blond guy with the thinning hair--the one who wore suits, what was his name—

GAYLE. Bernard.

JEN. (Overlapping.) No, no, no--It was before I moved in here. It was two years ago, in Philadelphia. That was why I left Philadelphia.

ELLY. You left an entire city because of some guy?

JEN. I had to.

GAYLE. How long were you and he—

JEN. Three years.

ELLY. Three years? Three *years*? You? I'm sorry, I'm not trying to be as insulting as I'm sounding, but--you know, as long as I've known you--you don't exactly settle into relationships.

GAYLE. Going out with a married man is not exactly settling in.

JEN. No, it's not, is it? I was his mistress. Pretty weird, huh?

GAYLE. How did it happen?

JEN. You know how those things are. I don't know. I was his paralegal, right? And we're like--together all the time, we go to the law library together, we go to court together, we go to lunch together, we take a road trip to Pittsburgh together, and--you know? One thing leads to another. I'm not going to explain it. Shit happens.

ELLY. Three years?

JEN. Yeah, its was not good.

ELLY. So you had to move?

JEN. Yeah, it was like the only way to do it. So, here I am-- sleeping around.

ELLY. Yes, here you are.

GAYLE. Here we are.

JEN. Here we are!

ELLY. Here we are.

(Pause.)

JEN. I haven't thought about that for a long time. It makes me feel weird--like I was some kind of villain. I used to feel that way all the time. It's funny--you can go through your life making mistake after mistake, but you always know, these are just mistakes, everybody makes mistakes. Then one day you realize that you're in the middle of a mistake that's something worse. It's not just another mistake anymore; suddenly you're a bad person. And it's so weird, it--happens without your even knowing it.

GAYLE. You're not a bad person.

ELLY. No, you're not a bad person. Still, I wouldn't tell that story to Jessica if I were you.

JEN. Yeah, she'd try to get rid of me.

ELLY. No, she wouldn't. She'd keep you around and pray over you. She'd make you stay up late and have long, meaningful talks about Jesus and His forgiveness.

JEN. She'd probably make me go to church.

GAYLE. For that? That is nothing.

JEN. Oh, you got a better story?

GAYLE. What? No.

JEN. Yes, you do. Don't you? You do.

GAYLE. I do not.

JEN. Look at the guilt on that face.

ELLY. Gayle--what did you do? Gayle!

GAYLE. I don't know what you're talking about.

JEN. Come on, spill it. Come on...

(Pause.)

ELLY. Oh, forget it. She never does anything wrong.

GAYLE. Oh, Honey.

ELLY. *(Laughs.)* Time for more scotch! And another round of cigarettes... *(She pours scotch and passes the cigarettes, then the lighter, around.)* This is fun. We should do this more often. This is really fun.

JEN. Except I'm not getting drunk. This is not good scotch.

ELLY. Yes, it is. It's great scotch. It cost me twenty bucks.

GAYLE. It's hard to get drunk in the morning. I don't know why that is, but it's true.

ELLY. Well, we'll just have to keep drinking. Okay, Gayle: What did you do?

GAYLE. *(Deliberate.)* I had sex with a man for money.

ELLY. You're kidding.

(ELLY starts to laugh.)

JEN. You what?

GAYLE. I had sex with a man for money.

JEN. You mean, you were like--a prostitute?

GAYLE. Yes. I was like a prostitute. I mean, I wasn't walking the streets and I didn't have a pimp or anything, it was just the one guy. But I did--he said he'd pay me for sex, so I did it.

ELLY. That is incredible.

GAYLE. No, it's not. It would be nice if it was incredible, but it's just a normal, sick story.

(Pause.)

ELLY. Well, are you going to tell the normal sick story?

GAYLE. Okay. I was doing temp work at this marketing research company, right? And the head of the project started coming onto me. So I told him to leave me along and he said he thought it would be mutually beneficial for me to hear him out. So I did. And--he told me that he could put me down as a special consultant on the project, somebody he brought in, and get the company to pay me sixty dollars an hour instead of the $12.50 I'd get from the temp agency. Well, if you multiply that by 40 hours a week—

ELLY. My God. He wanted you bad.

JEN. Did he come through with it?

GAYLE. Yeah, I made him pay me half in advance, and then I got the rest at the end of the week.

JEN. You did it for a week?

GAYLE. Two weeks. It was a lot of money.

ELLY. You must be pretty good, Gayle.

(The laugh uproariously.)

GAYLE. Well, let's just say I was just willing to do alot for that much money. I made it worth his while to keep me on the payroll for an extra week.

JEN. (Calming down a little.) Oh, God. I'm sorry, I'm just-- you know? That sounds kind of disgusting.

GAYLE. It was kind of disgusting. It was also illegal; it was embezzling.

ELLY. What did you have to do?

GAYLE. I think I'll leave the details to your sordid imagination, if you don't mind.

ELLY. Oh, come on, you're leaving out the best part—

GAYLE. I'm not going to give you details, El! I'm not that drunk!

(Pause. JEN hands her the scotch bottle.)

JEN. Why did you do it?

GAYLE. I needed the money. That was really just it. I was stuck, I was tired of living in New York, I was tired of working in these stupid boring offices--I was sick of it. I was just a mess. And he was offering me so much money. I mean, it was enough to go back to school and finish my degree, so, thanks to this sleezeball, I am now a social worker. You know? I don't know. It kind of makes me sick to think about it, but I might do it again if I had to.

ELLY. Better not tell that to Jessica.

GAYLE. Oh, she knows.

ELLY. You're kidding. You told her? Why on earth would you—

GAYLE. We were friends. Back before you guys moved in when we were living with Neil and Karen. So one day I told her. I needed to talk about it. But she couldn't really handle it.

ELLY. What did she do?

GAYLE. She didn't talk to me for two months.

ELLY. What do you mean, she didn't talk to you?

GAYLE. She--didn't talk to me.

ELLY. What a bitch.

GAYLE. It's kind of an extreme story for someone like her. I should have known better.

ELLY. Don't defend her.

GAYLE. I'm not defending her. I'm just trying to explain. She's different from us, you know?

ELLY. Yeah, she's a bitch and we're not.

JEN. Did she try to kick you out?

GAYLE. You know, she can't really kick any of us out. I don't know why we're always speculating on this. Everybody's name is on the lease. As long as we pay the rent and keep the kitchen clean, she can't do anything.

JEN. Then why does it *feel* like she can?

GAYLE. Probably what we should do, is move.

ELLY. No way. There's three of us and one of her. *She* should move.

GAYLE. She was here first. If we don't like her rules, we should go.

JEN. Yeah, but the rent here is so *cheap.* If I had to find another apartment, I'd have to pay real rent, and if I had to pay real rent, I'd have to get a real job.

ELLY. Me too.

GAYLE. Me too.

JEN. Let's face it, we're stuck with her.

ELLY. There's got to be a way around this. *(To Gayle.)* She stopped talking to you?

GAYLE. Yeah, I told her this terrible thing, and... she left me alone.

ELLY. That would be a way to go. Do you think if I told her I was having an abortion she'd stop talking to me?

GAYLE. No.

ELLY. Why not? That seems like a fair deal to me. You confess your sins to her, so she leaves you alone. It worked for you. I don't see why you should get the deal and not me. I mean, I'm as much of a sinner as you are—

GAYLE. That doesn't have anything to do with it. She wants to get rid of you because you're a ringleader.

ELLY. I am not!

GAYLE. You are too! Look at this! You're depressed, so we're all drinking scotch!

ELLY. I didn't force scotch on anybody.

GAYLE. I know, it's just sort of natural with you. Remember when we buried Irving in the backyard? Remember how that drove her crazy?

ELLY. Yeah?

JEN. I liked that. I mean, that was really cool.

GAYLE. Your hamster dies, and in no time flat you've got the whole household in the back yard, digging a little grave underneath the statue of Mary, reading a definition of "hamster" out of the dictionary as a eulogy—

JEN. A small rodent, with large cheek pouches. Amen.

GAYLE. See? Jen even remembers the definition.

ELLY. So what? Irving was a great hamster, he deserved a ceremony to mark his passing. I don't see why she had to get so nasty about it.

GAYLE. She's jealous. That's the kind of thing she's always trying to do, get us all together for little functions--like that seder she planned. I mean, maybe if we all, you know, went along with her more—

ELLY. We all went to her fucking seder. It was boring. A Catholic throwing a seder--I mean, it's stupid—

GAYLE. I'm just saying—

ELLY. I know what you're saying! You're saying that I deliberately provoke her, that I act like some sort of rotten little rebellious kid around here—

GAYLE. No, I'm not—

ELLY. Yes, you are! And I do! I don't care! She fucking drives me crazy and I love getting on her nerves! And it's so fucking easy for me to do, I mean it's just a delight, frankly, to annoy that woman, because all I have to do is be myself, only a little more so. You know, all I have to do is leave a dirty pot on the stove, or suggest that we have lobsters for Thanksgiving, or get high in the living room, and she's seething—

JEN. Yeah, what Jessica needs is a good lay.

ELLY. Oh, you think there's a flaw in the perfect relationship? Jeffrey's maybe not so hot in bed?

JEN. She's not sleeping with Jeffrey.

ELLY. What? What are you talking about, she is too. He's here all weekend.

JEN. They sleep together but they don't have sex. Didn't you know that?

GAYLE. They sleep together but they don't have sex?

ELLY. They've been going out for four years. She's thirty years old!

JEN. Yeah, but it's some religious thing.

GAYLE. She told you that? When did she tell you that?

JEN. I don't know, about a year ago. She was complaining about all the guys I had over, and I said, well, you know, you have Jeffrey over every weekend. And she said, yeah, but they weren't having sex, and I was. So I said I didn't understand what that had to do with anything and she got mad so I just said okay, if I want to sleep with some guy I'll go to his place. I thought you guys knew.

ELLY. What a bitch.

GAYLE. El—

ELLY. I mean, that's sick, you know? Sleeping with Jeffrey for four years--and she's supposedly in love with him, right?--and not having sex? Don't you think that's taking the old Catholic notion of sin a bit too far?

GAYLE. I don't think it's any of our business.

ELLY. Why shouldn't it be our business? Everything we do is her business. She makes it her business if I drink Campbell's soup. And you can just bet this abortion is going to be her business; she'll probably try to have me arrested—

GAYLE. Come on, you can't tell her—

ELLY. You know what I hate the most about her? What I've always hated about her? She doesn't *hurt*. You know? She doesn't feel pain. She's so sure of everything in her life, it's like an armor with her, all that fucking Catholic righteousness. Can't you just see her in bed with him? I bet she sleeps naked except for a pair of panties. And anytime he goes for them, she gently holds out her little hand, chastises him nobly, saves herself for marriage and keeps the universe intact. It's that iron will, you know, keeping Jeffrey and the rest of us in place. Jesus, she's like some fucking medieval saint—

JEN. Elly, please, just forget it, okay? She's not here, and it's a nice day so let's just forget her and have scotch for breakfast—

(ELLY smashes the bottle away from her. It rolls off the table and onto the floor. JEN fetches it.)

ELLY. I don't want anymore scotch! Why do you think I'm drinking this stuff? I'm drinking it because I half believe her! We all half believe that bitch just because she's so fucking sure of herself and none of us have a clue!

(Pause. They ALL think about this.)

JEN. Yeah. You know, we probably *should* move out.

(They ALL look at each other.)

ELLY. The rent here—
ALL. --is *so* cheap.

(They laugh.)

JEN. Oh, well, You want some?

(She holds up the bottle. Pause.)

BLACKOUT

Scene 2
Men on the Telephone, Which Is Where They Belong

(It is a couple of hours later. GAYLE, ELLY and JEN have moved into the living room. Music comes up, "I Will Survive", by Gloria Gaynor. All three are dressed up in sunglasses, hats and scarves. GAYLE sings the lead while JEN and ELLY perform a complicated back up routine. At some point, the whole thing dissolves into chaos.)

GAYLE. "First I was afraid. I was petrified. Kept thinking I could never live without you by my side. But then I spent so many nights thinking how you did me wrong, and I grew Strong. I learned how to get along. And so you're back—"

JEN/ELLY. Do do do

GAYLE. From outer space.

JEN/ELLY. Do do do.

GAYLE. You just walked in da da da da with that sad look upon your face

ALL. I should have changed that stupid lock, I should've made you leave the key, if I had known for just one second you'd be back to bother me, go on now, go—

(Et cetera. They are ALL camping it up royally and well into the second verse when the phone rings.)

JEN. Shit.

(JEN dances over to the phone. GAYLE and ELLY continue singing.)

GAYLE/ELLY. I will survive! I will survivvveee...

JEN. Hello. *(Loud.)* HELLO? OH, HI, RICHARDSON. (Pause.) WHAT? YOU'RE GONNA HAVE TO--COULD YOU--Just a minute. You guys— *(She rolls her eyes and points to the stereo. ELLY dances over and turns it down, but she and GAYLE continue to dance and sing with each other somewhat softly. JEN returns to the phone, but her mind is more on the music. She speaks loudly to be heard over the music.)* Sorry... No, we're just sort of hanging out... Elly and Gayle... What? I don't know, I'm kind of into hanging out here... Huh? *(She covers the phone and rolls her eyes at GAYLE and ELLY. ELLY dances over and gives her a drink.)* God. He wants to come over. Bigtime.

ELLY. No way. I cannot fucking deal with Richardson today.

JEN. *(Into phone.)* What?... no, I don't--Elly's not feeling very well...

ELLY. Don't lie to him. I feel fine. I just don't want to see any men.

JEN. No, we're just hanging out. Listening to records and shit...

GAYLE. We're bonding. Tell him we're female bonding.

JEN. *(Getting irritated.)* What... Well, we can talk tomorrow at work. We'll have lunch... Okay, fine, I know, but today's not good... I know what I just said, Richardson, you don't have to repeat it back to me. I just want to--What could be so fucking important--*(Snapping at ELLY.)* COULD YOU TURN THAT OFF FOR A SECOND? *(ELLY turns the music off. She and GAYLE watch JEN. JEN continues into receiver.)* Now, what is it?... Well, I'm sorry but you're getting on my last nerve here... Well, if you're not going to even tell me what it is you want to talk about I don't see why I should--... Yeah? What about it?... Well, I did, I thought you were completely off base, I'm not going to apolo—

ELLY. Hand up on him

JEN. *(Unbelieving, into the phone.) What?* You have got to be kidding... I don't care what you think, that is the craziest thing I've ever heard... No way. No... WHAT?... First of all, I didn't say that, but—

ELLY. HANG UP ON HIM!

JEN. RICHARDSON, YOU ARE A TOTAL LOON AND I AM NEVER GOING TO SLEEP WITH YOU... Oh yeah, then what are you saying?... You know what your problem is? You are fucking neurotic. *(She slams the phone down and stares at it.)* What an asshole.

ELLY. I never could stand him.

JEN. WHAT A FUCKING ASSHOLE.

(JEN paces furiously for a moment.)

GAYLE. What did he say?

JEN. I can't believe he just did that to me!

ELLY. He's crazy. How many times have I told you he's crazy?

JEN. Do you know what he just said to me? He just told me--you're not going to believe this. We had lunch Thursday, right?

GAYLE. Yeah?

(ELLY grabs the bottle of scotch and pours drinks, then passes ice around while JEN tells her story.)

JEN. So we're sitting there in the cafeteria and this Chinese guy, Billy, we know him from the mail room, he comes up and asks if he can eat with us. So I say of course, not realizing that stupid Richardson is *mad* at Billy for reasons which are completely beyond my imagination. So Billy sits down and Richardson starts sniping at him, this poor Chinese guy who can't even speak the language. And he's getting pretty loud, you know, everyone's sort of looking at us? So I say, you're getting kind of aggressive here, Richardson, and Billy's just smiling away because he doesn't even know what's going on, and Richardson tells me he's not being aggressive, he's being *assertive*--isn't that just perfect, it's like straight out of fucking therapy, you know? Christ. So I said, I think you're confusing assertiveness with machismo here, Richardson. And you know what he just told me on the phone? He wants to get together to talk about this because I was making like this personal statement about his fucking sexuality, and that means something like I've been lying to him all along and subconsciously I want to sleep with him. *(ELLY starts to laugh.)* It's not funny! You know, I think going into therapy was the biggest mistake of his life. His stupid therapist keeps telling him to let it all out. I'm sorry, but I don't think Richardson should let it all out. Doesn't it worry you that there are all these therapists out there telling weirdoes to just let it all out?

GAYLE. Oh, God, Something else to worry about.

JEN. You know what he said to me last week? He told me I was afraid of my sexuality. I use casual sex as a shield against real sex. That's what he told me.

GAYLE. What's real sex?

(ELLY and GAYLE are laughing hysterically.)

JEN. I'm not kidding. He gets all this shit from his therapist.

GAYLE. Has he told you you're a lesbian yet?

JEN. I think he's building up to that.

ELLY. Why do you hang out with this lunatic?

JEN. I don't know. He tells good stories. He's nice—

ELLY. Excuse me, but this is not nice!

JEN. Okay, he used to be nice. Before he went into therapy he was all fucked up, but he was really nice.

ELLY. Well, he's not nice anymore. You should just tell him to fuck off and die.

JEN. I can't do that. He's in love with me.

(ELLY starts to laugh.)

JEN. I knew you would do that. *(Protesting.)* He says he's in love with me. I feel awful about it.

GAYLE. That's not love.

JEN. What would you call it?

ELLY. Who cares what you call it; it's totally bizarre. Stay away from him.

JEN. I can't just dump him. I feel bad.

ELLY. It's not your fault he fell in love with you.

JEN. Yes, it is. Isn't it? I mean--isn't it, kind of?

GAYLE. Did you lead him on?

JEN. Who knows? I probably flirt with him sometimes, but—

ELLY. You flirt with everybody.

JEN. That's what I mean! So maybe I led him on. But I don't think so. I mean, I am *so* not interested in him. Anytime he brings it up, I just tell him face to face: I don't want to be insulting, but I am not interested in sleeping with you.

GAYLE. What does he say to that?

JEN. I don't know, some bullshit. You know what he did last week? He went around and asked all these people if they thought I was in love with him. It was like he was collecting opinions for a case. And everybody said yes. Can you believe that? They said *yes*.

ELLY. Who did he ask?

JEN. He wouldn't tell me. So I said: Look, Richardson, if all these people think I'm in love with you its because I really do *love* you. But you don't always fall in love with people you love. Shit happens, or it doesn't.

ELLY. I don't know why you're so nice about it. He's a serious loon. He's dangerous.

JEN. He is not.

ELLY. The only thing he'll understand is total rejection. Stay away from him.

JEN. Oh, that's nice. That's real compassionate.

ELLY. In the 20th century, compassion is a luxury you cannot afford. Unless you're getting off on this—

JEN. Mind you own business, Elly! *(Pause.)* I was really awful to him on the phone. Shit

GAYLE. He left you no choice!

JEN. I didn't have to yell at him. I mean, I just--I don't think it's his fault he's crazy. I think his parents fucked him up when he was little.

GAYLE. You think they abused him?

ELLY. Hold it right there. I don't want to have this conversation. I don't care what happened to him when he was four years old. Whatever it was, it doesn't give him the right to do these totally bizarre things to Jen. I mean, everyone has their reasons, even Jessica has her reasons, but that does not mean we have to go along with every weird, sick thing that they do.

GAYLE. Oh, come on. I thought you were into reasons. I thought that was all you wanted out of life--a couple of good, solid *reasons*.

ELLY. What?

JEN. That's right, before, when you were screaming about having an abortion, you said—

ELLY. That was different. And I was not *screaming*.

GAYLE You said that if Jessica and Roger could give you decent *reasons* you wouldn't have an abortion—

ELLY. I know what I said! I was talking about a different kind of reason.

GAYLE. Oh, please—

ELLY. Those kind are *rational* reasons, the kind you use like in arguments and talking about issues and stuff. This kind of reasons, Richardson's reasons, are just psychological excuses for totally off the wall behavior.

JEN. You always do this. You, like, make up these rules about what everything means—

ELLY. I'm not saying Richardon's reasons aren't valid; I'm just saying they're twisted and I don't want to hear it!

JEN. Oh, that makes a lot of sense. Valid but twisted. I get it.

ELLY. LOOK. Here we have little Adolph Hitler, right? And his mother hits him a billion times and his father hits his mother, and his uncle teaches him that--I don't know, that Jews murder babies and drink their blood, and God knows what else the Hitlers do, but what with one thing and another, little Adolph decides he's got to murder six million Jews. OKAY? DO YOU GET IT? EVEN ADOLPH HITLER HAD HIS

REASONS, BUT I DON'T CARE, THAT DOESN'T EXCUSE WHAT HE DID!

(Pause.)

GAYLE. God. Hitler is always such a conversation stopper. *(They ALL start to laugh again.)* It's true. Anytime things start to get a little messy, someone says, well, what about Hitler? And everybody shuts right up.

ELLY. Well, what can you say? The man was a monster.

JEN. Yeah, it's a good thing he never went into therapy. Think of what would have happened if some therapist told him to "let it all out." *(They ALL laugh. The phone rings.)* Oh, God, It's Richardson. Oh, shit.

ELLY Just don't talk to him. I'll get it.

JEN. No wait, not wait--what are you going to say?

ELLY. I'm going to tell him to fuck off and die.

JEN. NO, you can't—

ELLY. I'm kidding. I'll tell him you're in the shower.

GAYLE. Oh, that's a great idea. He'll believe that one.

ELLY. I'll tell him you're drunk. I'll tell him four of your old boyfriends come over and you all got drunk and now you're upstairs fucking your brains out so you can't come to the phone.

JEN. Oh, God, he'll just tell me I'm doing it because I'm afraid of my sexuality—

GAYLE. Are you going to answer it? I'll answer it.

ELLY. I want to answer it!

JEN. No wait--tell him--tell him--I went out.

ELLY. Oh, that's a great excuse. Very specific.

JEN. Tell him I went out for donuts.

ELLY. I'm just going to tell him you don't want to talk to him!

(ELLY picks up the phone.)

JEN. Elly, no—
ELLY. Hello? *(Pause.)* He hung up.

(ELLY sets down the phone. They ALL look at it for a moment.)

JEN. He hung up? He couldn't hang up.
ELLY. What do you mean, he couldn't hang up? He hung up.
JEN. Then it wasn't Richardson. He lets the phone ring for about 20 times before he hangs up.
ELLY. Is that who that is? He's the one who does that?
GAYLE. Didn't you know that? Don't you answer it?
ELLY. Not when I don't feel like it.
JEN. Why don't we have a phone machine?
ELLY. Jessica thinks they're immoral.
GAYLE. Come on, it's not that she thinks they're immoral. She just doesn't want to spend the money until she finds the exact right one.
ELLY. Oh, the exact right phone machine. What is the exact right phone machine?
GAYLE. One that's made of wicker. *(They laugh.)* Who do you think it was?
JEN. He'll call back.
GAYLE. It might be a she.
JEN. No, it's never a she around her. Only boys call us. None of us have any girlfriends.
GAYLE. That's ridiculous.
JEN. It's true!

GAYLE. My mother calls.

JEN. Oh, come on, you can't count mothers.

ELLY. Why not?

GAYLE. We don't have girlfriends? That can't be true.

ELLY. Wait a minute, Sarah calls me all the time.

JEN. She's your boss.

ELLY. Yeah, but she's my friend, too.

JEN. You can't count her.

GAYLE. It's not true that only men call here. It's just true that those are the only calls you count.

JEN. You're right. Oh, well, What can I say? I like men better than women.

ELLY. Jen! What are you doing saying things like that? Haven't you ever heard of feminism?

JEN. Of course I've heard of feminism. It really put me in touch with my feelings, and what I feel is, I like men better than women.

GAYLE. Isn't that interesting? I think they're mostly shitheads.

ELLY. I know.

GAYLE. I can't stand them.

ELLY. I know. They're such idiots.

GAYLE. Everything is their fault.

(They break up laughing.)

ELLY. Why are we laughing? It's true. *(They laugh even harder. ELLY reaches for the bottle of scotch.)* Oh, you guys. We're running out of scotch.

JEN. What do you mean. We have a lot—

ELLY. No, no, no. We're running low. I'll go get more—

(ELLY crosses to the stairs.)

GAYLE. Elly--no, Elly, you can't go out; you're drunk.
ELLY I AM NOT DRUNK!
JEN. How can you not be drunk? I am completely smashed—
ELLY. I AM NOT DRUNK!

(ELLY disappears into her room.)

GAYLE. You can't go out! We can't let her go out in this condition. She'll get arrested.
JEN. Can you get arrested for being drunk?
ELLY. *(Off.)* I AM NOT DRUNK!

(ELLY staggers back on, carrying a full bottle of scotch.)

GAYLE. You are so drunk. You are totally looped.
ELLY. I am not looped. I am tight. That's what they call it in Hemingway novels. Tight. I am tight.
JEN You are schnockered.
ELLY. No, you are schnockered. I am—
GAYLE. Blitzed.
ELLY. I am TIGHT! I am tight and Gayle is--trashed.
GAYLE. No, I'm not. I'm--wasted.
ELLY. Okay. I am tight, and Jen is schnockered, and Gayle is wasted. That's pretty good.
JEN. I don't want to be schnockered. I want to be--Wait a minute. You have another bottle?
GAYLE. You have another bottle? You bought two bottles?
ELLY. I felt it was an emergency.

JEN. Wait a minute! You shouldn't be drinking at all! You're pregnant—

GAYLE. Jen—

ELLY. No, no, hey, it's okay. That's *why* I'm drinking. Because I'm pregnant. I'm trying to anesthetize the little fella. *(Talking to her stomach.)* How's it going in there? Have you passed out yet? You won't feel a thing.

JEN. You think it's a boy?

ELLY. Honestly, Jen, I've heard of cradle robbing, but really—

JEN. Yes, ha ha, very funny. Seriously, you think it's a boy?

ELLY. I don't know, I guess--yeah. I think it's a boy.

JEN. You should have him. There's a shortage of men, you know. Some girl could need him someday.

ELLY. I can't have a baby. What would I do with a baby?

JEN. I don't know, I just—

GAYLE. You would raise him, you moron. People do it all the time.

ELLY. I don't know. Sometimes I think I do want to have a baby. I want to have, like, a baby and a dog. We could go places together. Elly and her baby and her dog. The Elly Team. I think that would be nice. *(Pause.)* Shit. I want a baby.

JEN. Then have it!

ELLY. I can't have it. I'm too fucked up.

JEN. You'll sober up.

ELLY. That's not what I *mean.*

JEN. Well, if you're going to do the abortion thing, you better take a couple of bodyguards along. You can get killed going into an abortion clinic these days. Those Right to Lifers are dangerous. Huh. That's kind of ironic, isn't it?

ELLY. It's occurred to people, Jen.

JEN. Well, at least it's still legal. If Bush had won the election, the three of us would probably be sitting here, trying to figure out how to operate a coat hanger.

ELLY/GAYLE. Oh, God, that's--Jen—

JEN. What, it's true!

GAYLE. I don't want to talk about politics.

ELLY. Especially in such graphic detail. *(She starts to open the bottle then stops herself.)* You know, I really don't want any more scotch.

GAYLE. Me neither. Time to make COFFEE.

(GAYLE tries to stand and can't.)

JEN. You know what we should do? We should make cookies.

GAYLE. *Cookies.*

JEN. We could make oatmeal cookies.

GAYLE. Oatmeal cookies...

JEN. This is great. I've decided: Getting drunk and making cookies is the perfect thing to do on a Sunday afternoon.

GAYLE. Sunday afternoon... *(Pause. She sits bolt upright.)* SHIT. It's Sunday afternoon. *(She leans over quickly and reaches for the phone. She picks up the receiver, stares at the phone for a second, then sets down the receiver. Then she picks up the receiver again.)* Shit.

(Pause. GAYLE sets the receiver down again. JEN and ELLY stare at her.)

ELLY. Is something wrong?

GAYLE. NO. No. What time is it?

ELLY. (Looking at her watch.) Quarter after twelve.

GAYLE. SHIT. What time was that phone call? The one we didn't answer?

JEN. It was, like, ten minutes ago. What, you think it was for you?

GAYLE. What? No, no, I just--nothing. I don't know. You know?

ELLY. You were expecting a call?

GAYLE. No. I mean, maybe. I don't know. Shit.

JEN. Yes you were. You were expecting a call from a man.

GAYLE. No. I just--I forgot about something.

ELLY. Call him back.

GAYLE. Who was it?

GAYLE. It wasn't anybody.

ELLY. Gayle!

GAYLE. What?

ELLY. You always do this.

GAYLE. I'm not *doing* anything.

ELLY. Oh, come on. Why can't you just tell us—

GAYLE. There's nothing to tell. It was just--nothing. Forget it.

ELLY. I thought alcohol was supposed to make people talk.

JEN. Leave her alone, Elly.

ELLY. Don't you trust us? *(Pause.)* Oh, great. That makes me feel just *great.*

(The phone rings. GAYLE jumps.)

ELLY. Gee, I wonder who that is? Probably nobody. It's probably not even worth answering. It's probably nothing.

(The phone rings again. GAYLE stares at it.)

JEN. Gayle! Answer it!

(GAYLE quickly picks up the receiver.)

GAYLE. Hello?... Oh, hello. Oh--I'm not sure. Just a minute, I'll check.

(GAYLE covers the receiver with her hand and looks at ELLY. Pause. ELLY reaches for the phone.)

ELLY. Hello?... Hi. *(Pause.)* Yeah, I'm sorry too. It's just-- this is really weird for me--What? I can't hear you, you have to--*(Pause.)* I can't right now. I just need to--I need to think for a little while, okay? *(Pause. The phone call becomes progressively more difficult for her. She covers her face with her free hand.)* Yeah, yeah, I'm still here. It's just--*(Pause.)* Roger, we can't talk about this over the phone--*(Pause.)* I know, but I just think you're getting--*(Pause.)* I don't know. It doesn't sound like a real good idea to me--Well, because marriage is serious, my God, that's not something you just dive into. You were always the one with commitment paranoia. *(GAYLE and JEN stand to leave. ELLY gestures them to sit down.)* You guys-- *(Into phone.)* What? Roger, this is too serious to decide over the phone. I am not going to decide to marry you over the phone. *Yes, I know that abortion is serious too, I never said it wasn't--* Fuck. Fuck. Look. I don't want to marry you. Okay? I don't want to marry you, Roger. I don't want to spend the rest of my life with you. I don't want to have your child. Okay? Okay? I don't want to marry you. I am not in love with you OKAY?

*(GAYLE and JEN look at each other, and begin to leave again.
ELLY reaches out and grabs GAYLE's hand to stop her.
She leans against her suddenly, cradling the phone against
her chest.)*

BLACKOUT

Scene 3
Gods and Mothers

*(The lights are lowered and the blinds are drawn. A half filled
plate of oatmeal cookies sits on the floor in front of the
couch next to a disgustingly full tray of cigarettes. The easy
chair has been dragged over to the couch, and JEN and
GAYLE sit holding a Ouija board on their knees. ELLY
lounges full length on the couch and watches them. The
cursor moves rapidly across the surface of the board.)*

JEN. You're pushing it.

GAYLE. I'm not, I swear!

JEN. N--E--Y--Barney. We're talking to Barney, is that
right?

GAYLE. *(Watching board.)* Yes.

JEN. I have never had a Ouija board work this good.

GAYLE. What do you want to ask him? Hi, Barney.

ELLY. Barney? We're talking to a male spirit? Wouldn't
you know. Tell Barney we don't want to talk to men today.

JEN. Elly, no--shit, she doesn't mean it, Barney. Are you
still here? *(She watches.)* Yes. Thank God.

(ELLY giggles.)

JEN. Stop it, Elly. This is very serious and if he thinks you're a nonbeliever he'll go away. You can't just fool around with this.

ELLY. Okay, okay. I have a question. Ask him--if Gayle's new boyfriend is going to call back.

GAYLE. Elly—

JEN. Yes. It says yes.

GAYLE. You're pushing this—

JEN. I would never push a Ouija—

ELLY. I knew it! I knew it was a guy.

GAYLE. It was just a date.

JEN. Come on, come on, we have to ask him another question. Think of a question.

Gayle. I want to know--let me think, I want to know—

ELLY. Is there sex in the afterlife?

(The cursor moves wildly from one end of the board to the other.)

JEN. Great. Oh, great. That's what it does when it knows there's an unbeliever present. Barney, no, we believe in you.

ELLY. No, we don't, Barney.

GAYLE. It's saying something. Look, it's spelling something.

JEN. God, we didn't even ask a question. This is amazing—

(Pause. They ALL watch.)

GAYLE. Go.

JEN. Go. Go where?

ELLY. Go fish.

JEN. Elly—

GAYLE. No, come on, pay attention, it's saying go outside and do something--it's a beautiful day out—

JEN. Wait a minute. You are pushing this, aren't you?

GAYLE. Of course I'm pushing it! For heaven's sake, let's get out of here! We've been lying around all day—

JEN. That's great. That's just great. You guys are both jerks.

(JEN starts to throw the Ouija board back into the box.)

ELLY. No, come on, come on, I want to ask it a question.

JEN. Just forget it, Elly. You made your stupid point.

GAYLE. Look, I'm sorry. I just thought—

JEN. You shouldn't fuck around with this, I'm telling you—

ELLY. I'm not fucking around. I have a question. I want to know--I want to know if I can use this thing to talk to my mother.

JEN. Oh, ha ha, that's real funny.

ELLY. I'm not kidding!

JEN. You can only talk to dead people with a Ouija board, moron.

ELLY. No kidding, moron.

(Pause. GAYLE takes her hand off the cursor and looks at
  JEN. They ALL look at each other.)

GAYLE. Oh, Jesus, Jen. You're kidding, right?

JEN. Your mother's dead? When did she die?

ELLY. What? Four years ago. Are you kidding? She died four years ago.

JEN. Your mother's dead? You didn't tell me you mother was dead.

ELLY I've been living with you for a year. How could you not know?

JEN. Why didn't you tell me?

(Pause.)

ELLY. That is so depressing.,

JEN. Well, we don't exactly see each other a lot. Just weekends and shit.

ELLY. Yeah. It just makes you wonder. I mean, who knows what kind of shit we don't know about each other?

JEN. God, I know. I mean, like, think about it. How did we meet?

ELLY. God help us all. Jessica picked us.

JEN. That's my point. The three of us, we could be anybody, you know. I saw this movie, where this girl got a roommate through the personals, who tried to *kill* her—

GAYLE. Jen!

JEN. What?

GAYLE. Come back.

JEN. Oh. Sorry. *(Pause.)* So--how'd your mom die?

ELLY. Oh--she was killed in a car accident. Some moron ran a red light at 50 miles an hour and smashed into her. He was driving this Oldsmobile station wagon, and she was in a Chevette. She didn't stand a chance.

JEN. Do you miss her?

ELLY. Oh, yeah.

JEN. That's nice. I mean, it's not nice that she's dead; it's nice that you miss her. If my mother died I think I'd have a party.

GAYLE. Jen!

JEN. What? My mother's a bitch!

GAYLE. Well, my mother's a bitch too, but I wouldn't throw a party.

ELLY. My mother was cool.

GAYLE. Yeah?

ELLY. Yeah. She was very loving and compassionate and she loved being a mother. And--she was very spiritual, you know—

JEN. Jesus. She sounds like Jessica.

ELLY. What?

GAYLE. I don't want to talk about Jessica again...

ELLY. SHE WAS NOTHING LIKE JESSICA

(Pause. Both JEN and GAYLE are a little startled at the force of this outburst.)

JEN. Jesus.

ELLY. I just don't see how you can say that.

GAYLE. El, would you calm down? You've been flying off the handle all day.

ELLY. My mother listened to people! She *listened*. And she understood that we are all fucked up. The entire planet. She used to say, we're all sinners—

JEN. Yeah, I've heard that. Jessica says that all the time.

ELLY. But when Jessica says it, she means that we're sinners and she's perfect, and when my mother said it, she meant that we're all a little fucked up and it's no big deal.

GAYLE. *(Irritated.)* Look, I wasn't kidding. Do you think we could stop trashing Jessica for maybe, I don't know, five or ten minutes?

ELLY. Oh, I'm sorry. That's right, you and Jessica are such close friends. Ever since way back when—

GAYLE. I just don't think she's all that bad.

ELLY. She is too.

GAYLE. She is not! If she were, she wouldn't bug you so much.

ELLY. She bugs you too.

GAYLE. She does not.

ELLY. She does too!

JEN. You guys—

GAYLE. She does not! I admire the woman—

ELLY. She is a self righteous prima donna!

GAYLE. Yeah, well, so are you.

(Pause. They look at each other for a moment, then ELLY looks away, stung.)

JEN. Do you guys want a cookie? *(Pause.)* How about some more coffee? I want more coffee...

(JEN exits to the kitchen for coffee.)

GAYLE. I'm sorry. I just think, you know, that you're pissed off because you're pregnant and you're taking it out on Jessica.

(ELLY picks up a knife and begins to play with it.)

ELLY. Oh, no, my dislike for her is very sincere. Every night as I go to bed, I fantasize about skewering her in any number of ways, like one of those medieval saints she's so fond of imitating. You know, after living with her, I'm starting to understand why they all ended up the way they did.

GAYLE. All right. It's a given, you hate her. Why don't you move out? Just move out.

ELLY. Real job, real rent.

GAYLE. You could get a real job and pay real rent, El. You're thirty years old! It's not unheard of!

ELLY. Hey. I'm an American. We're a nation of professional adolescents. Why buck a trend?

GAYLE. Because life is passing you by.

ELLY. No, I'm passing it by, remember?

(JEN reenters with coffee.)

GAYLE. All right, let's talk about that, then. You're pissed off about this baby.

ELLY. On the contrary. I delight in the knowledge that my reproductive system actually works. After all these years of fooling it, I've wondered.

JEN. How did you get pregnant, anyway? I mean, nobody gets pregnant anymore. *(They look at her.)* Nobody who doesn't want to, I mean. A little bit of birth control goes a long way.

ELLY. The diaphragm, if used properly, is 98% successful. Well, meet Miss Two Percent.

GAYLE. And that doesn't make you mad.

ELLY. No. Because it doesn't matter. I'm going to have an abortion, and that's that.

GAYLE. What would your mother think about that?

ELLY. My mother is dead.

GAYLE. What would she think, El?

JEN. She would hate it. She was Mother Earth Goddess, remember?

GAYLE. Jen—

JEN. I just think you should stop playing shrink. I'm just sitting here waiting for you to say, "El--let it all out...".

GAYLE. All right.

JEN. I mean, personally, I think abortion is a bad idea, but if she doesn't want to talk about it—

ELLY. You do?

JEN. God, yes.

ELLY. You?

JEN. Are you kidding? After what I've learned about babies this year, I would never have an abortion.

ELLY. Great.

JEN. Babies are big business.

ELLY. Oh, no.

JEN. Oh, yeah. Everybody wants one. They were kind of cheap for a while, but the ceiling has really come off in the past couple years. We did five surrogate mother contracts, just this month.

ELLY. This does not help me.

JEN. Listen, all sorts of shit goes on nowadays. I know a guy who set up this deal where he got a pregnant teenager to give her baby up for adoption to this very nice yuppie couple in exchange for medical and living expenses during the pregnancy. Bill came to $50,000.

GAYLE. That isn't legal.

JEN. Oh, grow up. There are plenty of ways around the law, and the market is so hot right now no one really knows what's going on. So the way I look at it, if you don't want this kid, you could make somebody else real happy and end up with a few bucks in the bargain.

ELLY. Sure. Everybody wins.

JEN. You could quit your job. Now, here is a way around the recession. With one of these deals, you really could quit your job. Take a few months off, get some desperate sterile couple to foot all the bills...

ELLY. You could set up one of these deals for me?

GAYLE. El!

ELLY. I'm kidding! I could never sell my baby. I'd rather kill it. *(Pause.)* That's what I love about contemporary society. Options.

JEN. Oh, come on, that's not what I said.

GAYLE. You said, babies are big business.

JEN. Yeah, but you're making it sound sleazy. It's a good thing.

GAYLE/ELLY. Jen!

JEN. What? I'm just being realistic! We live in a market economy. Money is power. Now babies are money, so babies are power. You guys are the ones who are always screaming about women's rights and rah rah feminism, well, that's fine but I'm telling you, I've been working in law offices for four years now and those guys are not going to just hand over their money and their power and their little offices. No way; they live for that shit. Now all of a sudden, these guys have decided they want babies, too--they want something we've got, right? So all I'm saying is: Let them pay for it. And you can both stop looking at me like I crawled out of the woodwork somewhere. I make a lot of sense and you know it.

ELLY. Oh, you do. I'm just wondering how come you're so

practical about some things and such a moron about Richardson.

JEN. Would you leave Richardson out of this? He's none of you business. I swear to God, you're obsessed—

ELLY. I just think he's—

JEN. I already told you, I don't care what you think!

GAYLE. You guys, come on, Richardson's got nothing to do with whether or not Elly should sell her baby.

JEN. I didn't say sell! I said put it up for adoption for a profit.

GAYLE. Fine. I'm disgusted either way.

ELLY. I'm not. I think it's kind of funny. Babies for cash. I can't wait till they start advertising. I could do a lot with this. Buy a baby and build a family--shoot for an upper, middle upper consumer... 50 thou isn't that big an investment--it's much cheaper than a house—

GAYLE. Okay, we get the point.

ELLY. You realize, of course, that this could put abortion clinics out of business. The Right to Lifers will win, not because they're right, but because having babies became economically feasible! But they won't care! Because in the embrace of capitalism and morality, ALL ARE WINNERS! WE HAVE ACHIEVED UTOPIA! YES! YES! YES!

(ELLY laughs maniacally, then falls into natural laughter again. Both stare at her.)

GAYLE. Are you all right?

ELLY. Don't you think it's funny?

GAYLE. No.

ELLY. How could you not think this is funny? We were

laughing at Hitler before. If Hitler is funny, this is funny.

GAYLE. I never said Hitler was funny.

ELLY. You were laughing.

GAYLE. I was not—

ELLY. Laugh, Damn you! It's funny! LAUGH.

(ELLY jumps her and tickles her viciously. JEN joins in. GAYLE screams laughs for a moment, then they collapse in a heap on the couch.)

JEN. God. Do we have any aspirin?

ELLY. Or alka seltzer?

GAYLE. I'll get it.

(GAYLE goes to the kitchen. ELLY stands and wanders to the window.)

ELLY. We should go outside, it's so nice--*(Pause.)* Shit. Hey, hey, what kind of car does Richardson drive?

JEN. Oh, please, please could we not talk about him? Please?

ELLY. No, no kidding, Jen, I think—

JEN. Gayle, she's doing it again!

(GAYLE reenters with ginger ale and aspirin.)

GAYLE. Cut it out, El.

ELLY. No, listen—

JEN/GAYLE. *(Overlapping.)* SHUT UP! CUT IT OUT!

ELLY. All right, but don't blame me—

JEN/GAYLE. *(Overlapping.)* SHUT UP!
ELLY. *(Overlapping.)* ALL RIGHT!

(For one instant, everyone is screaming simultaneously. They start to laugh, then pass around the aspirin.)

ELLY. I still want to talk to my mother.

JEN. Your mother probably went to heaven, or whatever you want to call it, so we're not going to be able to get her on the Ouija board. The Ouija board is for low-rent spirits.

GAYLE. What did you want to tell her?

ELLY. I don't know. I wanted to tell her how much I loved her. And I wanted to tell her that I'm all fucked up.

JEN. You could pray to her.

ELLY. What? Come on, that's stupid.

JEN. Why is that stupid? I don't think that's stupid at all. It might be stupid for me to pray to my mother because she's alive and she's a drunk and I hate her, but you really loved your mother.

ELLY. I hate God. *(Pause.)* I hate God for killing my mother.

GAYLE. Some moron in an Oldsmobile station wagon killed your mother.

ELLY. You think I haven't told myself that a billion times?

(Pause.)

JEN. So why pray to some stupid God? Pray to her.

ELLY. What if she doesn't answer?

JEN. She will.

ELLY. Jen—

JEN. No, you can't feel stupid. Come on, we'll all pray to

her. Okay. Let's see. We should all hold hands.

    ELLY. Jen, come on.

    GAYLE. No, I want to do this, too.

(GAYLE sits and grabs ELLY'S hands.)

    JEN. Okay, okay, we have to close our eyes.

    ELLY. You guys—

    GAYLE. CLOSE YOUR EYES!

(They do.)

    JEN. Okay--now, Elly, you have to tell us what she looks like so we know who we're praying to.

    ELLY. Well--um, okay. She had blonde hair and brown eyes--her hair was long, kind of, and straight--and people used to say I looked like her, but I don't think I really did. And she used to wear this funny little hat, it was kind of like this little fisherman's cap, you know--*(Pause.)* I can't, Jen.

    JEN. That's okay, that's good enough. Okay. Here we go. *(Calling.)* Mrs. Stewart—

    GAYLE. No, you can't call her Mrs. Stewart. You have to call her Mom.

    JEN. Oh, right. Okay. *(Calling.)* Mom--Mom, we're down here and we're fucked up and we need to talk to you!

    GAYLE. We're confused, Mom!

    ELLY. And we're a little drunk! I'm pregnant, Mom!

    GAYLE. Things are a mess!

    ELLY. We need you to tell us that we're okay, Mom!

    GAYLE. We need some advice!

    JEN. We need courage! We need support!

ELLY. Mom, are you there?
GAYLE. Mom?
ALL. (Calling, in unison.) Mooooommmmmm!
JESSICA. (At doorway.) Just what is going on here?

(Pause. ALL of them open their eyes and look at her. JESSICA stares at them. JEN and GAYLE are somewhat abashed; ELLY is suddenly defensive. Freeze.)

BLACKOUT

END OF ACT I

ACT II

Scene 1
What's He Doing Out There?

(It is a few seconds later. JESSICA stares at the mess.)

JESSICA. What are you doing? Look at this place!

(JEN and GAYLE scramble to clean.)

JEN. *(Overlap.)* Shit. Sorry, Jessica—
GAYLE. *(Overlap.)* Jessica--I'm sorry about the mess. It's not as bad as it looks. We didn't expect you back this early—
JESSICA. *(Overlap.)* Look at this place! What did you guys do, sit around and drink all day? Oh, God, you've been smoking in the house--you guys—
JEN. Not very much. We were mostly smoking outside. We just, it's just that we brought the ashtray in, and it was full of cigarettes--shit, I'll just go get the air stuff—
GAYLE. *(Overlap.)* Things just got away from us a little; we'll clean it right up—
JESSICA. Oh, forget it. It's okay, Gayle--GAYLE, IT'S OKAY. I don't care. Jen--forget it.
JEN. Forget it?
JESSICA. It's fine, we can clean it up later. Listen, Richardson's out front. He's across the street in his car. He wants to talk to you.
JEN.What?

57

(JEN crosses rapidly, angrily to the porch.)

JESSICA. He came by to talk to you because he said yo had a fight or something. I told him I'd tell you he was out there.

JEN. *(Overlap.)* He WHAT? That jerk--Oh, that is just fucking great. This is unbelievable.

JESSICA. No, now come on, you're just getting all... *(Calling.)* He just wants to talk to you--why are you overreacting like this? He just said that you had some sort of disagreement and he wants to...

ELLY. *(Overlap.)* Aren't you mad about this?

JEN. *(Screaming from porch.)* WHAT IS HE DOING OUT THERE? What a dweeb. I mean, what a fucking weenie. It's not enough that he has to follow me around the office like some kind of retarded shithead, now he's got to, what, park on my street? This is an invasion of privacy, an invasion of my private fucking spaces, you know? Shit. I mean it, I say we arrest him. This has to be illegal. WOULD SOMEONE PLEASE PAY ATTENTION TO ME? GAYLE! ELLY! SOMEBODY CALL THE FUCKING COPS!

GAYLE. *(Overlap.)* We'll clean this right up—

(GAYLE picks up several dishes.)

JESSICA. (Overlap.) Gayle, it's okay, leave it. Apparently we have a disaster on our hands. Richardson looks like death warmed over--What did she do to him? Is she sober?

ELLY. She's fine.

JESSICA. She certainly doesn't sound fine.

(GAYLE crosses to the door, JESSICA following. They ALL pile out on the porch and stare off at Richardson.)

JEN. Can you believe this?

GAYLE. He's just sitting there.

JEN. He's such a jerk

ELLY. What is the big deal? I say we ignore him.

GAYLE. Isn't he even going to get out of his car?

JEN. Okay, Jessica, what did he say?

JESSICA. He said he wanted to talk to you.

JEN. If he wanted to talk to me, why didn't he come to the door? I mean, *normal* people come to the door.

JESSICA. I didn't ask.

ELLY. Ignore him. Believe me, this works with men.

GAYLE. Wait a minute. He's getting out of the car. He's -- no, he's just tying his shoe or something.

JEN. What else did he say?

JESSICA. He didn't say anything else. I told him I'd send you out. He's very upset.

JEN. Well, so am I. This is totally off the wall.

ELLY. Yo! RICHARDSON.!

(ELLY waves wildly.)

JEN. Elly! Stop it!

ELLY. I'm just trying to get him to wave. He won't even look at us.

JEN. I thought you wanted to ignore him!

ELLY. I changed my mind.

GAYLE. He looks bad. He kind of looks like a zombie, doesn't he?

JESSICA. *(Overlap, to JEN.)* Do you want to change? Maybe you should change.

ELLY. Jessica, would you cut it out? She looks fine.

GAYLE. How long do you think he's been out there?

JESSICA. Well, he was there when I got home. I talked to him for a few minutes and then I pulled around the corner, so—

GAYLE. That's not what I mean. I mean, he was just sitting there, right? So he could have been there all afternoon for all we know.

ELLY. He's been there at least fifteen minutes; I saw him.

JEN. Why didn't you tell me?

ELLY. I tried! You told me to shut up!

GAYLE. So he's been out there for a while. God. If you hadn't come home, he might have stayed there all night.

ELLY. He looks like he's about to start sprouting things. Moss. Mushrooms.

(GAYLE starts to snicker.)

JESSICA. I don't think—

ELLY. I know, I know. It's not nice to make fun of crazy people. I'm sorry.

JESSICA. Richardson isn't crazy. He's upset. Jen—

JEN. DON'T PRESSURE ME. I'm thinking! *(Pause.)* He is such a shithead.

JESSICA. I thought you cared about him.

JEN. Of course I care about him!

ELLY. That's not the issue.

JESSICA. If you love a person you don't put him through this kind of pain, no matter what he said or did in the middle of a fight. Besides, you were drinking—

ELLY. Oh, come on—

JEN. Shut up, Elly.

(JESSICA crosses and sits with JEN.)

JESSICA. I'm not trying to pressure you. I've had my share of fights with Jeffrey, and I know how awful they can be, but I think it's a mistake to let this go any further. You and Richardson have been close for a long time, and I don't think either of you wants to sacrifice that.

JEN. I know, it's just--he kind of scares me.

GAYLE. Jessica. If she's scared of him—

JESSICA. What is there to be afraid of?

JEN. I don't know. Nothing.

ELLY. Why don't you leave her alone?

JESSICA. I happen to think she could use a little help.

ELLY. It just seems to me that Jen is perfectly capable of deciding for herself what she wants. I mean, she's not one of your little high school students, you know?

(Pause. JESSICA stands up and begins to cross to the door.)

JESSICA. Fine. I'm sorry I said anything.

(JEN stands, alarmed.)

JEN. Where are you going? Jessica!

JESSICA. I'm going to tell Richardson you don't want to talk to him. That's what you want, isn't it?

JEN. I don't know what I want!

JESSICA. Look, I told him you would come out and talk to him. I didn't realize it was going to be such a catastrophe.

JEN. I'm sorry but—

JESSICA. If you don't want to talk to him, I think he needs to know that, so he doesn't wait around anymore. Is that all right with you?

JEN. No, come on, that'll just make him mad--Oh, Geez.

(JEN stands immobile, confused.)

GAYLE. Jen, don't do anything you don't feel comfortable doing.

JEN. Oh, come off it, Gayle! You're sounding like a therapist again and it doesn't help, you know?

JESSICA. (Overlapping.) What are you afraid of? He loves you very much—

JEN. Would you just stop saying that word? Jesus!

ELLY. He doesn't love her—

JESSICA. I don't think you know anything about it.

ELLY. I don't know anything about love?

JESSICA. Elly--I only meant you don't really know Richardson well enough to say that.

ELLY. And you do.

JESSICA. I think I know him better than you do, yes. We've talked.

ELLY. Wait a minute. Wait a *minute*. You talked to him?

JESSICA. Yes, I like Richardson and sometimes I talk to him. Is that all right with you?

ELLY. That depends on what you said. Did you tell him she was in love with him?

JESSICA. What?

ELLY. Richardson went around taking a poll, asking everyone if Jen was secretly in love with him. And he tells Jen that everyone said yes. Were you in on that?

JESSICA. I don't know anything about a poll. All I know is he's been very upset about the fights they've been having, so we had lunch last week, and—

ELLY. You did. You told him she was in love with him.

JESSICA. I told him the truth. Jen obviously loves him much more than—

(JESSICA stops herself. Pause.)

ELLY. Than all the men she fucks? You realize, of course, that that's what he wants. All he wants is to fuck her. And that's what the whole problem is: She won't fuck him.

GAYLE. El, for God's sake.

JESSICA. I don't think you know anything about it.

ELLY. I think I do.

JEN. You had lunch with him? You mean--you've been talking to him behind my back?

JESSICA. I wasn't trying to interfere. He's your boyfriend; I respect that. I was only trying to help.

JEN. (Overlap.) HE IS NOT MY BOYFRIEND! HE HAS NEVER BEEN MY BOYFRIEND, HE WILL NEVER BE MY BOYFRIEND. Did he tell you that? Did he tell you he was my boyfriend?

JESSICA. I don't care what you call it—

JEN. I care what you call it!

(JEN stands suddenly and stomps off the porch.)

ELLY. Jen, come on, don't--Jen!

JEN. MIND YOUR OWN BUSINESS, ELLY! GOD. Both of you--I wish you would both mind your own business once in a while.

(JEN exits. They watch her.)

JESSICA. I hope she doesn't hurt him.

ELLY. What? You hope *she* doesn't hurt *him*?

JESSICA. Elly, come on, would you calm down? This isn't the end of the world. I mean, I'm not asking her to marry him. I just think they should talk to each other.

ELLY. You can't talk to him.

JESSICA. Of course you can. I talk to him all the time. He's weird, but he's not crazy.

ELLY. He *is* crazy.

JESSICA. He is not!

ELLY. He's off the deep end. He calls her 60 billion times a day to scream at her; that is not, to my knowledge, the way sane people behave—

JESSICA. He calls her up and screams at her because he's worried about all these men she sees. He's afraid she's going to get AIDS. If she hasn't gotten it already.

ELLY. She's not going to get AIDS.

JESSICA. Elly, come on! You know as well as I do that she's at risk!

ELLY. She says she's careful.

JESSICA. Careful isn't good enough anymore.

GAYLE. *(Looking off.)* Oh, God. She's getting in the car with him.

JESSICA. Why shouldn't she get in the car with him?

ELLY. Gayle, tell her what he's been doing!

GAYLE. Jessica--it's just that he seems so angry with her—

JESSICA. You've never gotten angry at someone you love?

ELLY. You know, you do--you keep saying that word like it's some sort of magic formula. It's like you think all this LOVE is going to solve something.

JESSICA. I'm not going to apologize for that.

ELLY. But the problem is, this thing between Jen and Richardson isn't about love, it's about sex, a subject you-- *(Pause)* haven't fully considered.

JESSICA. Maybe I haven't. And maybe I am too idealistic about those two. I just--I think they really love each other. I'd like to see them end up together.

ELLY. Do you even listen to her? She's not interested in him. She's said it a million times—

JESSICA. Yes, but that's not how she acts. You've seen them together. They're adorable.

ELLY. All they do is yell at each other!

JESSICA. That is not all they do. When they get along,, they're like a couple of kids. Remember when he was always bringing her lunch? He was sure she wasn't eating right—

ELLY. Yeah, she was on a diet and he kept bringing her macaroni and cheese. She was ready to kill him; she gained five pounds.

JESSICA. Well, she didn't have to eat it if—

ELLY. Oh, come on, who's going to say no to macaroni and cheese?

JESSICA. Now you're just being ridiculous—

ELLY. He's trying to control her!

JESSICA. Well, maybe she could use a little control in her life. And she's not the only one.

ELLY. I beg your pardon?

GAYLE. You guys--just don't go there, okay?

JESSICA. You're right. I'm sorry.

(JESSICA smiles at ELLY, who looks away and goes into the house.)

JESSICA. *(To GAYLE.)* I'm sorry. I'm not going to let her get to me today. I feel too good. What a day. It's almost like summer, isn't it?

GAYLE. It's better than summer. I love this kind of weather.

JESSICA. This is the end of it, though. It's supposed to freeze tonight.

GAYLE. Really?

JESSICA. That's what the paper said. And the trees are all pretty much past their peak.

(JESSICA turns her face to the sun.)

GAYLE. Did you have a nice drive?

JESSICA. It was great. Jeffrey and I went all the way up to Manchester and walked on the beach. When we started out this morning, we were only going to go as far as Andover, but the day was so warm we just kept driving. I had no idea it was so close. So we took our shoes off and went walking in the surf.

GAYLE. Sounds great.

JESSICA. It was. *(Pause.)* We had a good talk. *(Pause.)* We talked about getting married.

GAYLE. What? Jesus. Are you kidding? What is going on today? It's got to be the weather.

JESSICA. Thanks a lot.

GAYLE. I'm sorry. I didn't mean that the way it sounded. It's just--somebody else I know got proposed to today. I think it's kind of weird is all.

JESSICA. Well, he didn't--Jeffrey didn't propose—

GAYLE. Well, what did he say?

JESSICA. He just wanted to talk about it, you know--generally.

GAYLE. Generally?

JESSICA. Yes, generally.

GAYLE. Oh, Jessica--come on, is he doing this to you again?

JESSICA. What do you mean? I think we're ready to talk about marriage now; before it just wasn't the right time.

GAYLE. How long are you going to let him do this to you?

JESSICA. I don't know what you're talking about. We're just trying to work things out. We both think it's important not to rush—

GAYLE. I know, I know. I'm sorry.

(Pause.)

JESSICA. I guess I sound pretty defensive, don't I?

GAYLE. No, I shouldn't have said anything. It's just--I'm having such a weird day. *(Pause.)* Look, Jessica, I don't want to rain on your parade; I don't, but at some point don't you just have to give it up? I mean, I like Jeffrey; he's a sweet guy, and I know you love him, but he's been waffling for so long. Don't you just want to--I mean, some days, don't you just want to take *charge* of your life, give him his walking papers or an ultimatum or something, just take *control--(Pause.)* Don't you want that?

JESSICA. So--what are you saying? You think that breaking up with Jeffrey will give me control over my life? Is that what you're saying?

GAYLE. I don't know--yes. Yes. I think it would be a good thing—

JESSICA. So I break up with Jeffrey, and what happens then? Then I start looking around again? My friends fix me up, or I join one of those agencies?

GAYLE. No, that's not what--you don't have to do that shit.

JESSICA. Okay. Let's say I break up with Jeffrey and join a health club. Or take classes at UMass. Or start going to bars. I'm not going to do that, Gayle. I'm just--it's so humiliating. I won't do it.

GAYLE. You're a beautiful woman. You won't have any trouble finding someone.

JESSICA. It's not easy for me. It's never been easy. It takes me a long time to feel comfortable with people. And I don't have a lot of time anymore. All right?

GAYLE. You're only 30 years old!

JESSICA. I'll be 31 next month.

GAYLE. That's young.

JESSICA. Not if you want children. *(Pause.)* I want to have children. I've always wanted children. It's late for me; I can't-- I don't have a lot of years to keep looking anymore.

GAYLE. But--I mean--what if Jeffrey decides--Jesus, Jessica. He's been waffling for so long.

JESSICA. I don't know why we're even talking about this. I love Jeffrey. We just need time to work a few things out. That's what we talked about today; we're working things out and in a year or so we're going to get married. Gayle--don't look at me like that. This is one of the happiest days of my life. Why don't you believe me?

GAYLE. I do. I'm sorry, I just--I'm so confused today. On the one hand, 30 seems young, on the other hand, 30 seems old. I think we should all be getting on with our lives, and I have no idea what that means anymore. So what did Jeffrey say?

JESSICA. Well--it wasn't so much what he said. We were walking in the ocean, and the water was freezing; we were kind of laughing about that... and there was this little girl running up ahead of us, chasing the waves in and out--you know, how kids do--and she had this giant piece of seaweed that she was swinging around, waving over the ocean. She looked like she was blessing the waters. So we started talking about kids, and how there were probably kids all over the world chasing waves, playing with seaweed--the human connection felt so powerful. Thinking about all those people, all those children, on all those other shores. So we started talking about that, and--I don't know. He brought it up--we started talking about getting married. I guess that sounds a little crazy.

GAYLE. *(Dry.)* No. It sounds very romantic. Jeffrey's a very romantic guy.

JESSICA. Then when we were driving home, we took all these back roads to avoid the traffic, and we ended up driving through what must be the wealthiest suburbs in the country. It was appalling. I kept thinking about how the earth is being destroyed, about how many beaches aren't safe anymore because everything's getting so polluted because American capitalists cannot see past their wallets or their lovely little lawns--. I mean, how do you think these grand fortunes are made? They're built out of the ruined lives of South African blacks, or Brazilian peasants, or Korean factory workers. And I just wanted to stop and say to these people: We are sharing this planet. All of us, we're all in this together. You have no right to be doing what you're doing. I wanted to tell them to go look at that ocean. Do you know what I mean?

GAYLE. I'm--not sure.

ELLY. I have no idea what you are talking about.

(JESSICA starts. ELLY has stood at the screen door through much of JESSICA'S last speech. She crosses casually out onto the porch. Both watch her uneasily.)

JESSICA. The only reason they can live in these palaces is because halfway around the world someone is working 18 hours a day on a coffee plantation, or in some Godforsaken copper mine, or who knows what. Americans don't realize that in order to live this wonderful, opulent life, they have to destroy the rest of the world.

ELLY. I don't know. Maybe those people in the mansions aren't exploiting Brazilian peasants. Maybe they inherited their money and now--now they're running vast philanthropic empires from these modest New England estates. I mean, you never know.

JESSICA. Never mind. What did you do today, Gayle?

GAYLE. Well—

ELLY. Oh, this and that.

JESSICA. How could I forget. You had a seance. Honestly, Elly, I don't know where you get these ideas.

ELLY. It wasn't a seance; we were praying. And it wasn't my idea--it was Jen's.

JESSICA. What were you yelling? Mom?

(Pause.)

ELLY. Yes. We were praying to my mother.

JESSICA. Oh.

ELLY. We got an answer, too.

JESSICA. Really? Oh, no, look at this--when did this happen?

(JESSICA examines the hole in the wicker chair.)

ELLY. Who knows? Wicker's so fragile. We probably should have bought something more sturdy. Like plastic.

JESSICA. I'll get Jeffrey to look at it. He's learning how to do caning, did I tell you? He's making me a rocking chair. I'll take this downstairs, then we should probably get started on that living room. You guys made quite a mess.

GAYLE. We'll clean it up, Jessica.

JESSICA. I don't mind helping.

(JESSICA exits with the chair.)

ELLY. Can you believe that? She drives by somebody's house, a total stranger, and decides that they made all their money out of the blood and tears of South American peasants. She doesn't even know these people!

GAYLE. El, don't pick on her politics. She's right and you know it.

ELLY. And what is it with Jeffrey? Is the man trying to work out his sexual frustration in wood? This place is turning into American Arts and Crafts: We have the dulcimer Jeffrey made, the bookshelves Jeffrey made, the rocking chair—

GAYLE. Elly, would you just stop it? You are really driving me crazy.

ELLY. Me? What about her?

GAYLE. What about her? She walked in on us trashing the living room, holding a black Mass as far as she can tell, and all she did was offer to help us clean it up! Jessica is not the problem today.

ELLY. Oh, yes, she's just a saint. It was just saintly the way she sent Jen off with the Local Psychopath. That was very compassionate.

GAYLE. It's not going to hurt Jen to talk to him. Jessica's right, they should work this out.

ELLY. What is it with this About Face?

GAYLE. It's just--this is not a good day to pick a fight with Jessica. Apparently Jeffrey said something to her, I don't know what—

ELLY. I can give you an educated guess. "Please fuck me, Jessica, please—

GAYLE. Lay off it, Elly. I mean it. Leave her alone today.

ELLY. You know, those two really are perfect for each other. She won't have sex with him and he won't marry her.

GAYLE. I SAID LAY OFF.

ELLY. Right. Lay off. Saint Jessica comes home, and everybody falls right back in line. Just this morning, you were telling me what a bitch she was when you wanted to talk about this prostitution thing, but now—

GAYLE. God, I wish I'd never told you that.

ELLY. Why? I'm on your side!

GAYLE. Because I'm ashamed! I'm *ashamed* of what I did!

And Jesus, if there is a right side, it's hers. She had a right to condemn it.

ELLY. She was a total bitch—

GAYLE. She was right! What I did was not okay. I mean, we can sit here and say, oh, everybody makes mistakes, but that's no excuse. A mistake is not something you just ignore, as if it never happened. A mistake is a mistake, you know? Jessica had a right not to like it.

ELLY. No one has a right to condemn another person like that.

GAYLE. You've been doing it all day!

ELLY. That's different.

GAYLE. Forget it. I just don't want to fight anymore, okay?

ELLY. She fucking thinks she's better than us—

GAYLE. Well, maybe she is!

ELLY. God, you are such a wuss; she walks in the door and you turn into jello! "Oh, she's so much better than us—"

GAYLE. Fuck you.

ELLY. Yeah, fuck you too.

GAYLE. Forget it. I am not getting caught in the middle of this anymore.

ELLY. You live here. You are in the middle of it.

GAYLE. I AM NOT GOING TO LET YOU DO THIS TO ME!

ELLY. You let her do it. You listen when she trashes me. You had a whole household meeting about throwing me out over a can of soup!

GAYLE. Yeah, and maybe we should have done it.

ELLY. Yeah, maybe you should have. *(Pause.)* You know what gets me? You both--you and Jen--you'd rather live with me. But even so, if it came to a choice--she would win.

GAYLE. This is not a war—
ELLY. Yes it is.

(ELLY crosses and looks through the screen door.)

GAYLE. Elly, please. *(Pause.)* I'm warning you—
ELLY. FUCK OFF.
JESSICA. *(Calling as she enters living room.)* Who's going to do the dishes?
ELLY. *(Cheery.)* I will!

(ELLY returns to the living room. When she speaks her manner is quite friendly. GAYLE follows her, somewhat confused and wary.)

JESSICA. Oh--that's okay. I'll do them.
ELLY. It's our mess. I'll do them.
JESSICA. It's no trouble.
ELLY. Do you want to do them?
JESSICA. Sure. I don't mind.
ELLY. I know you don't mind, but do you want to do them?
JESSICA. Yes. I want to do them.

(JESSICA picks up glasses.)

ELLY. Then why did you ask who was going to do them?
JESSICA. It was just a rhetorical question.
ELLY. "Who's going to do the dishes" is a rhetorical question. I see.
JESSICA. I'll do them; I don't mind—
ELLY. But I'll feel guilty if you do them. I'll do them.

(ELLY reaches out and takes the glasses from JESSICA, who does not give them up immediately. For a moment, the two women stand with their hands on the glasses, then JESSICA lets them go. ELLY stands before her, holding the glasses for a moment, but JESSICA turns and begins to put together the Ouija board. GAYLE crosses quickly and takes it from her.)

GAYLE. I'll get that, Jessica.

(JESSICA nods and starts to move furniture back in place. ELLY sets down the glasses deliberately, crosses to stereo and drops in a tape. The Temps, "Just my Imagination" comes on. She dances for a moment, Jessica watching and becoming more and more impatient. JESSICA finally picks up the glasses and goes to kitchen.)

ELLY. *(Sweet.)* Jessica, I said I'd do the dishes. This is our mess. You really should let us clean it up.
JESSICA. I don't mind.
ELLY. But I told you I'd get them.

(ELLY takes glasses from her and crosses to the kitchen.)

JESSICA. Just--be sure to do the glasses first. If you do them last, they spot because the water gets dirty.

(Pause. ELLY exits.)

JESSICA. I'm always afraid to say something; she's so defensive. But honestly, its like she doesn't even see the dirt. I hope we can get some air in here before it gets too cool. This place smells awful.

(JESSICA props open the screen door; she and GAYLE clean for a moment. ELLY reenters, crosses to the cassette and snaps it off.)

ELLY. Jesus. The Temps can be so fucking sentimental.

JESSICA. Oh, don't turn that off. I love that song.

ELLY. *(Muttering.)* Tough shit.

JESSICA. I beg your pardon? *(Pause.)* Did you hear me? I like that song.

ELLY. So?

JESSICA. Eleanor.

ELLY. What did you call me?

GAYLE. Listen Elly, I like the Temps. Jessica likes the Temps. When Jen comes home we'll see how she feels about them. But the best you could hope for is a split decision, so for now could you put them back on?

ELLY. Jessica, I have to tell you something.

GAYLE. El—

ELLY. Gayle, you said you didn't want to be in the middle of this. So stay out of it. Jessica, yesterday morning I found out that I'm pregnant, and I've decided I'm going to have an abortion. I know you don't approve, I know you probably think that it's murder or something, but--I'm going to do it, and I'm not apologizing for it. I've decided that it's not a good idea to get too apologetic about who you are. So--that's why I'm telling you this. Everybody says your baby is a part of you; well, this abortion is a part of me, and I want you to know about it. *(Pause.)* Okay, that's all. That's it. I'm done. *(Pause.)* Aren't you going to say anything?

JESSICA. I'm sorry.

ELLY. Jesus Christ.

JESSICA. *(Pause.)* What did Roger say?

ELLY. He doesn't like it.

JESSICA. I'm not surprised.

ELLY. What do you mean, you're not surprised? Have you been having lunch with him, too?

JESSICA. No, I just--I was remembering the day he brought his little niece over here. He was very sweet with her. I thought he would be a good father.

ELLY. Well, if you want to know the truth, the thought never crossed his mind until last night, when I smacked him across the face with the imminent possibility.

JESSICA. But he wants to have this baby—

ELLY. Yes, Roger wants to marry me and set up house, although I'm sure you and everyone else cannot imagine why. I'm the one. I don't want to marry him. I am not in love with him.

GAYLE. Elly, I don't think—

ELLY. I don't want to talk about Roger.

JESSICA. I don't believe that. I don't believe you don't love him. I've seen you together; you seem so happy. I mean--it's natural that you're frightened by this, but I'm sure it would all work itself out once you were married. Children are wonderful; when the baby is here, I'm sure—

ELLY. It's not that simple.

JESSICA. Do you not want children? You could put it up for adoption. So many people want children, Elly, so many really good people—

ELLY. That's not the issue.

JESSICA. Issue? What are you talking about, issues? This isn't about issues! We're talking about a child—

ELLY. No, we're not. It's not a child.

JESSICA. Then what is it?

ELLY. I don't know. It's not--look, I don't—

JESSICA. You don't want to do it. Why else would you be so unhappy about this? You just need some time to think.

ELLY. I don't have time.

JESSICA. You do. You won't have to go through this alone. We'll all be here for you. You could even--if you wanted to raise it yourself, if you needed to quit your job for a while—

ELLY. *(Overlapping.)* No!

JESSICA. *(Overlapping.)* You wouldn't be alone! I know--I know we haven't been getting along, but we could try. I know you're a good person—

ELLY. NO, I'm not a good person--please, God, please don't be nice to me!

JESSICA. You're just confused. You don't really want to do this—

ELLY. I do! I want to do this! I don't want this baby to exist in the world. I don't care how awful that sounds; it's the truth. I'm tired of the way my life is just happening to me, all this stuff just keeps happening. My job, wicker furniture, Campbell's soup, my boyfriend, who, I'm finally able to admit after much too much time, I don't love--it's all blurred together, and you think that some of this has got to be more important than the rest, but it gets to a point where you just can't make anything out. And I'm not saying that the world is a bad place to be; I'm not saying I wouldn't want a kid in the world. But my life is too blurred right now; it's like one of those bad dreams that just keeps going on and on and on and you just wish like hell that you'd wake up but it just keeps going; it's one cryptic, meaningless, confusing thing after another. But at some point, you have to say, hold it. Hold it. And I'm saying it now. A baby is not something that should just happen. This baby is not going to happen.

JESSICA. Elly--I understand.

ELLY. You do not; even I do not understand that and I said it. Look, I don't want to talk about this!

JESSICA. *(Suddenly steely.)* Well, I do. You brought it up, now you can just deal with what I have to say. This is not about me, or the fact that I see the world differently from you. You're not a child. You're confused, I understand that, but that's tough. Things do happen. Big decisions come up. And you don't just muddle through them and hope it all ends well! Your life *isn't* a blur. It's a life. You own it. And you're talking about denying that right to another human being. I know you're in pain, but if you just run away from this because you're hurt, or angry, or scared, you're never going to grow up. So stop whining and *deal.*

(JESSICA exits. Pause.)

GAYLE. Are you okay?

ELLY. Oh, Jesus. What if she's right?

GAYLE. Maybe you're both right.

ELLY. We can't be. We can't both be right, can we? God. How does anyone anywhere decide anything?

GAYLE. I don't know.

ELLY. She was so nice.

GAYLE. Yeah, she was. Why wasn't she nice to me? It would have made such a difference.

(Pause.)

ELLY. Aw, she's full of shit.

GAYLE. *(Pause.)* Come on. We have to finish cleaning this up.

(They stand and look at the mess for a minute, then at each other.)

ELLY/GAYLE. Nah.

ELLY. Lord. Look at this sunset. It's almost enough to make you believe in God.

(They go out onto the porch.)

ELLY/GAYLE. Nah.

ELLY. Gayle--who was this guy on the phone?

GAYLE. What?

ELLY. The guy who called today.

GAYLE. It probably wasn't him.

ELLY. You like him, huh?

GAYLE. He's just this guy from work.

ELLY. What's his name?

GAYLE. Phil.

ELLY. What's he do?

GAYLE. He's a shrink.

ELLY. You're kidding.

GAYLE. See, I knew you'd do this.

ELLY. You're going out with a shrink. Of course.

GAYLE. We're not going out. He just said he might call today.

ELLY. So why didn't you call him?

GAYLE. It was very tentative. It was no big deal.

ELLY. But he called—

GAYLE. It probably wasn't him. It was probably Richardson calling back.

ELLY. Call him back. Ask him out to dinner.

GAYLE. El, I'm not going to do that.

ELLY. You like him? What's he like?

GAYLE. He's nice. He's a nice guy.

ELLY. Yeah, but what's he like?

GAYLE. He's not a nerd, and he's not an asshole.

ELLY. CALL HIM UP.

GAYLE. See, I knew you were going to do this. That's why I didn't want to tell you.

ELLY. What? What am I doing? I'm telling you to call this nice guy on the phone, what's wrong with—

GAYLE. You're making a big deal out of nothing. He's just a guy, and you're working up this big romance here so if I ever do go out with him it's going to be totally anticlimactic.

ELLY. I'm just saying you should call him. How's he supposed to know you're interested—

GAYLE. I'd just like to wait and see what happens, okay?

ELLY. That's a mistake. I'm telling you. If you have a chance at something that might mean something to you, I'd take it.

(Pause.)

GAYLE. What are you going to do, El?

ELLY. I don't know *(Pause.)* Mom? I'm going to have an abortion. Mom?

(They look at the sunset, waiting for an answer.)

BLACKOUT

Scene 2
I'm Sorry, Violence Is Just Not Cool

(ELLY lies on the couch in semi darkness. The nearly full scotch bottle and a half glass of scotch sits on the coffee table. We hear Lou Reed singing "Busload of Faith".)

ELLY. "You need a busload of faith to get by... busload of..."

(JESSICA stands in the doorway, watches ELLY for a moment. She crosses into the room cautiously.)

JESSICA. Excuse me--do you mind if I turn the music down? I was about to go to bed.

ELLY. Oh, sure. I'm sorry.

(ELLY jumps up and turns off the stereo.)

JESSICA. Oh, that's--I didn't mean that you had to turn it off, I just—

ELLY. That's okay, I wasn't really listening to it.

(The BOTH stand awkwardly for a moment, then ELLY crosses back to the couch.)

JESSICA. Well. Good night.

ELLY. Jessica--I'm sorry I was so awful this afternoon. I was really out of line.

JESSICA. That's okay. You were upset.

ELLY. Still.

JESSICA. Would you like to talk about it?

ELLY. No. I really wouldn't.

JESSICA. It might help, it might really help you get some perspective—

ELLY. *No.* Thank you. I just--thank you. No.

(ELLY puts her feet up and picks up a magazine.)

JESSICA. I just meant--I'm sorry, could you take your feet off the couch, please? *(Pause. ELLY takes her feet off the couch.)* It's just--that fabric marks up very easily. And it's hard to clean.

(ELLY looks at her.)

ELLY. Sorry.

JESSICA. *(Chilly.)* Well. Goodnight.

(JESSICA exits. ELLY shakes her head, takes a hit off the scotch, leans back and puts her feet back on the couch. She

*hears someone on the back porch, sits up, and looks. JEN
enters, staggering against the doorframe in the darkness.
ELLY reaches for the light.)*

ELLY. Oh, Jen. Hi.
JEN. No, Elly, it's okay, don't turn on the light. I'm fine—

*(ELLY has snapped the light on. In the light, severe bruises
can be clearly seen on JEN'S face. She supports herself
against the door for a moment.)*

ELLY. Oh, my God. Oh, Jesus, Jen.
JEN. I'm okay.
ELLY. *(Very upset.)* Oh, fuck. Oh, shit—

(ELLY stands and brings JEN to the chair.)

ELLY. Sit down, Jesus--oh my God, he hit you—
JEN. I'm okay. I'm gonna be fine.
ELLY. Shit. GAYLE! Oh, God, Jen, what do you need? Do
you need anything? Yes. Ice. You need ice. Oh, shit. GAYLE!
COME ON! GAYLE!
JEN. Elly, don't, there's nothing you can do about it now—
ELLY. Yes, we can, we can put ice on it and call the police
and have the fucking asshole castrated, sweetheart--Oh, God,
look at you. GAYLE!
JEN. Elly, I'm okay. He didn't rape me or anything, he just
hit me.
ELLY. *(Bitterly sarcastic.)* Oh, well, yes, that is something
to be grateful for. GAYLE!

(JEN leans back and touches her face gently as ELLY dashes to the kitchen. GAYLE appears in the doorway in a robe. She looks at JEN for a moment, stunned. ELLY returns, fumbles with ice and a dishcloth.)

ELLY. Here. Put this on--I don't know, put it on your eye, I guess--

JEN. It's okay. I'm okay, Elly.

GAYLE. What happened?

ELLY. Gayle, what do we do? You work in a hospital, do this--

GAYLE. I'm not a nurse, I'm just a social worker--

(GAYLE crosses and helps with the ice.)

JEN. Ouch. Be careful.

ELLY. Sorry. Jesus. I told you, I *told* you he was dangerous--

JEN. He just hit me.

ELLY. He hit you A LOT.

JEN. Well, yeah, he hit me a lot. What a jerk.

GAYLE. Have you called the police yet?

ELLY. We were just getting to that.

(ELLY crosses to the phone. JESSICA enters.)

JEN. Elly--

JESSICA. What's going on--oh, my God. *(JESSICA stands immobile in the doorway.)* What happened?

JEN. Richardson and I got into a fight.

JESSICA. Oh, look at you--come on, you have to lie down.

JEN. Could I just have some aspirin? I have a splitting headache.

(GAYLE crosses to the kitchen and returns with aspirin and water a few moments later.)

JESSICA. Is anything broken? Did you pass out or anything?

JEN. No, and it's a miracle. I'm telling you, the last thing you need after drinking all day is a bash in the head.

JESSICA. Richardson did this?

ELLY. All that love that he feels for her burst forth in a rapturous outpouring of abuse. You know how love is.

JESSICA. What happened? He's so gentle—

ELLY. Yes, he's a very gentle psychopath.

JESSICA. Who are you calling?

ELLY. The police.

JESSICA. The police--Don't you think we should find out what happened first?

ELLY. No, I think we should call the police first.

JEN. Elly, come on, I don't want to call the police.

GAYLE. Jen, we have to take you to the hospital and get you checked out. They're going to want to know what happened.

JEN. I'm not kidding, no cops!

JESSICA. Okay, okay, it's okay--Elly for heaven's sake, put the phone down—

ELLY. We can't take care of this ourselves, Jessica. She's been assaulted.

JESSICA. We don't know that.

ELLY. What do you mean, we don't--what do you mean?

JESSICA. I just want to find out what happened before anyone goes flying off the handle!

ELLY. You want to know what happened? TAKE A LOOK

AT HER. THAT ASSHOLE ASSAULTED HER. What do you think, she assaulted him?

JESSICA. *Please don't yell—*

GAYLE. Would you two shut up so we can find out what happened?

JEN. I don't know what happened! I mean it was weird, you know. You know how Richardson is. He hardly ever makes total sense. You can say to him, like, A B C, Richardson, and he'll say something like--110. 43. I don't know.

GAYLE. Where did you go after you left here?

JEN. Yeah. You know, I didn't want to go anywhere with him. I went out there and told him to totally leave me alone; I told him I was really tired of how weird he was getting and I never wanted to talk to him again. I did. And he said I wasn't being fair because you don't just cut off friendships like that. So I said the problem is, you don't want to be my friend, Richardson, and he said we couldn't talk about it here because you guys were watching us. So--Jesus.

GAYLE. So you went with him.

JEN. I thought I owed it to him. We've been friends for two years.

JESSICA. Then what happened.

JEN. Then we went out to dinner. We went to Christopher's. And that was okay for a while, because he was talking about other things--I mean, he kept talking about this guy Billy from work and what Billy did, and the kind of people he hung out with--and finally, I said, I don't really think Billy is the issue. And he said he just wanted to warn me about Billy because he thought he had AIDS. And that made me kind of mad, because first of all I don't think it's true, and second, I'm not going to sleep with Billy. I mean, it's not like I sleep with every man I know. So I said that and we started arguing again, and Richardson got so loud the manager came over and asked us to leave.

GAYLE. My God.

JEN. No kidding. It was really embarrassing and kind of scary, you know? So we were standing in the parking lot and I said look, I'm going home, and he said--He said we still had to talk. So--we went back to his apartment.

ELLY. Jesus, what were you thinking?

JEN. How was I supposed to know he'd do this?

JESSICA. What happened then?

JEN. Well--we got inside, and he got really uptight.

ELLY. He got *more* uptight.

JEN. Yeah. His roommate wasn't there, he told me that about twelve times. And then he kept sort of hovering around me and asking me what I wanted. It was really weird, he kept saying, What do you want? What do you want? And I said, you know, a cup of tea, maybe? I mean, I didn't know what was going on. Oh, boy. So he got mad at me and he said I was being cruel to him, so I said, Richardson, just get the tea, I just want some tea here. And he said, what about what he wanted. He said nobody cared what he wanted. And I said that wasn't true, that I did care, I said that was why I was even there, because I cared about him. So then he kissed me. And I let him. I let him, just for a second, because--I don't know why, I just--then when I tried to get out of it he freaked out, he--do I have to tell you this part?

GAYLE. No, it's okay, we get the picture.

JEN. He's such a fucking shithead.

GAYLE. I know. It's okay.

JEN. I've been stuck in his apartment for three hours. I

locked myself in his stupid fucking bathroom for three hours while he sat out there and told me he was sorry. Three solid hours.

ELLY. How did you get out?

JEN. He left finally. I told him I wasn't going to come out until he left. *(The phone rings.)* It's him. Don't answer it. *(JESSICA crosses to the phone.)* Jessica, please don't answer it!

JESSICA. Hello? *(Pause.)* Yes, she's here. She's--she's going to be fine. *(Pause.)* I don't think that's a good idea. She's upset. *(Pause.)* Yes, I know. I'll tell her. *(Pause.)* Please, don't-- I know. I know. I'll tell her. We'll call you back. *(She hangs up.)* He's very sorry.

ELLY. We are calling the cops.

JESSICA. I don't think that's necessary.

ELLY. The hell it's not. He tried to rape her and now he's calling to say he's sorry? Well, I'm sorry too, but we're calling the cops and making sure he never comes near her again.

JESSICA. He didn't try to rape her.

ELLY. What would you call it?

JESSICA. It certainly was not rape and getting hysterical about this is not going to help anyone. *(Pause.)* I mean, I'm as sorry as anyone that this happened, I really am, and I'm not excusing Richardson; there is no excuse for what he did, but—

(Pause.)

ELLY. But?

JESSICA. Nothing. I think we should all go to bed now. We're all upset, and tired, and I think we should talk about this in the morning.

ELLY. Talk about what in the morning? What's to talk about?

JESSICA. I just think we should go to bed.

ELLY. Well, I just think we're a little too wound up to go to sleep right now. So I want to hear what you have to say. You obviously have something to say. I want to hear it.

GAYLE. Jessica--what is it?

JEN. I want to hear it, too. I mean, I told you what happened. What, do you think I'm lying or something? Is that what you think?

JESSICA. No, of course not. Of course not, Jen--it's just, a few things aren't clear to me. That's all. We'll talk about it in the morning.

JEN. What? What's not clear? What did that asshole say to you? I told you what happened! What did he say?

JESSICA. He didn't say anything. He was crying, he was apologizing. He said it was a misunderstanding. He just kept saying that.

ELLY. A misunderstanding. That's great. "Oh, look, my fist is in your eye, I just can't understand how it got there—"

JESSICA. *(Snapping.)* Please don't make jokes about this; there is nothing funny about this!

(Pause.)

ELLY. I'm so sorry. You were going to tell us about Richardson's misunderstanding.

JESSICA. I guess I just--I think they misunderstood each other.

JEN. What do you mean? I didn't misunderstand anything. I was trying to be nice to him, so he hit me! You explain it; it's Richardson's dazzling logic—

JESSICA. Jen, you said it yourself, you let him kiss you.

My God. What do you think that said to him?

JEN. It was just a kiss! I felt sorry for him!

JESSICA. Don't you think that misled him?

JEN. I don't know! Maybe, but I didn't mean--look, I told him a million times—

JESSICA. You told him you cared for him, you kissed him—

JEN. I told him—

JESSICA. *(Overlap.)*--and he took that to mean you would sleep with him. Can't you understand why he thought that?

ELLY. I knew that's what you were thinking.

JEN. Elly, shut up, I can defend myself. I don't have to defend myself. *He* hit *me.*

JESSICA. I'm not accusing anyone.

JEN. Then what are you doing?

JESSICA. I'm just saying--I think you both made mistakes.

ELLY. And what was her mistake? I missed that part. What did she do to him?

JESSICA. I think she knows.

JEN. No, I don't. I don't.

ELLY. We don't know, Jessica. You're going to have to tell us.

GAYLE. That's enough. We have to stop this before somebody says something we all—

ELLY. *(Overlapping.)* Let her say it, Gayle. *I want to hear her say it.*

JESSICA. How do you think he feels? How do you think he's felt all these years while she's been just stringing him along? You don't know, you never bothered to think. I know. I know! He loves her; he wants a life with her and she--she just tramples on that like it's nothing, like it's--Well, I'm not surprised he finally--if you want to know the truth, I'm surprised this didn't happen sooner. She brought this on herself with all these games she plays. Sex is not a game.

ELLY. *(Pause.)* What do you know about sex?

(PAUSE.)

JESSICA. I don't think my private life has anything to do with this.

ELLY. I think it's got a lot to do with it.

JESSICA. Well, I don't choose to discuss it with you.

ELLY. I wasn't giving you a choice. You don't give us choices. I mean, we boycott soup because you say so, not because we choose to. We bought all that fucking wicker because you said so. I'm just saying. Living in this house isn't always about choices, is it?

JESSICA. I can't believe this. If you're unhappy here, this is hardly the time or the place to discuss it.

ELLY. This is exactly the time and place, but that's not what we were discussing. We were talking about you, and sex and control. We were talking about your remarkable observation that Jen was asking for this because she sleeps around.

JESSICA. I never said that.

ELLY. Oh, you said something pretty damn close, Jessica; it flew right out of your mouth and we all heard it. And I was just wondering what it is in your life that plants these ideas in your head when you see your roommate sitting in front of you with a black eye.

JESSICA. I don't have to answer you.

ELLY. We told you he was dangerous. We told you and told you, all three of us, and you wouldn't listen.

JESSICA. Yes, I know you would love for this to be my problem; well, it's not my problem.

ELLY. *(Overlap.)* You can't stand the idea that you were actually wrong about that lunatic, so this has to be her fault! Reality has to conform to you! Where the hell do you get off?

JESSICA. You're ridiculous. You're hysterical and ridiculous—

ELLY. You're so pure, you're so *right,* you're the fucking virgin mother, aren't you? And we're just a mess! But you love that; we're just you own little chorus of sinners that you keep around because we make you feel so fucking pure.

JESSICA. That's enough—

ELLY. No, it's not enough. It's not near what I have to say to you—

GAYLE. *(Overlapping ELLY.)* Really, really, you guys. She's hurt, could you just...

JESSICA. You can't stay here.

ELLY. What?

JESSICA. I know you're going through a hard time right now, but this is just--too much. I don't have to listen to anymore of this. I want you out tonight. Do you hear me? Tonight.

(JESSICA starts to push by ELLY to leave the room. ELLY suddenly picks up a small, sharp knife from a cheeseboard on the coffee table and raises it calmly, at a distance from JESSICA. There is an uncertain, shocked pause.)

ELLY. Yes, you do have to listen to this.

GAYLE. Elly, stop it. EL.

JEN. Jesus Christ, Elly, have you lost your mind?

(ELLY closes in on her as JESSICA tries to back away.)

ELLY. On the contrary. I'm just in the middle of a misunderstanding, Jessica and I have misunderstood each other, and then she provoked me, and now I'm going to hurt her, but then we're all going to forget about it because it was really her fault to begin with. That's the way it works, isn't it?

JESSICA. STOP IT—

(JESSICA tries to bolt away from ELLY, but ELLY grabs her arm and brings the knife up before her face. JEN and GAYLE bolt forward, then hand back.)

JEN/GAYLE. Elly--Elly, Jesus Christ--ELLY.

ELLY. What do you think? Should I hurt you, Jessica? Will it help? If I hurt you, will you understand that you are one of us? You're just as bad as we are, Jessica. YOU. ARE ONE. OF US.

GAYLE. Elly, put the knife down. PUT IT DOWN.

(Suddenly bewildered, ELLY backs away from her, then drops they knife on the coffee table.)

ELLY. What am I doing? What am I doing?

(PAUSE.)

GAYLE. Jessica, are you all right?

JESSICA. No. I'm not. I'm not.

ELLY. Jessica— *(JESSICA suddenly bolts from the room. ELLY starts after her then stops. Pause.)* Oh, shit.

JEN. I cannot believe you did that.

GAYLE. That was weird.

JEN. Did you see that?

GAYLE. I saw it.

ELLY. I just pulled a knife on my roommate. That is really no way to behave.

JEN. You were excellent, Elly.

ELLY. Jen! My mother did not raise me to act like this!

JEN. Oh, come on, it wasn't a sharp knife. Besides, she was really being a bitch.

ELLY. I can't believe I did that!

JEN. *(To GAYLE.)* Wasn't that excellent?

GAYLE. Well, "excellent" isn't the word that popped to *my* mind—

ELLY. What was I doing? What did I say to her? I pulled a knife on her! How could I do something like that?

GAYLE. Elly. It's okay. You didn't hurt anybody.

ELLY. I have to go talk to her.

GAYLE. I don't think that's a good idea.

JEN. No, hey, I think she heard you. Pick up a knife, and everybody listens.

ELLY. Well, we have to do something!

GAYLE. We will do something, just give me a minute to figure out what!

ELLY. I'm going up.

GAYLE. Elly, no, if anyone's going up there, it's not you—

(GAYLE turns to go upstairs just as JESSICA enters the room. She wears a light coat over her pajamas and carries her bag. The two women back away slightly, watching each other cautiously.)

JESSICA. I need my keys. My car keys. I left them on the bookcase. *(Pause.)* Please get out of my way.

ELLY. I'm sorry, Jessica. I don't know why I did that. I just lost it. You were hurting Jen, you were blaming her, and I just—

JESSICA. That's not why! That's not what you said.

ELLY. No. I guess it wasn't.

JESSICA. All those things you said. They're not true. You don't know me. Both of you, you just trample on everything I value. You throw it away as if it were nothing, as if it were dirt, and then you expect me to just applaud you, to say, yes, that's fine, that's wonderful, throw it away, I don't care! This man loves her, he--I know, I know I was wrong about him he's troubled, he's--I was wrong. But he loves her so much, and I--Jeffrey and I--I'll never have that. You think I don't know? You could have a child. And you want to kill it. I may never have that, and you--let me by!

(ELLY does. JESSICA gets her keys.)

ELLY. Where are you going? Are you going to Jeffrey's? You can't go over there.

JESSICA. You attacked me!

ELLY. Oh, come on, it wasn't a sharp knife! (Beat.) Well, it wasn't. I shouldn't've done it, but we're all making mistakes tonight. Let's just calm down and work this out. I can't believe these words are coming out of my mouth...

GAYLE. She's right, Jessica.

ELLY. I am, Jessica. Come on. We're all in this together, so could we just—

JESSICA. No. We're not. I'm not one of you, and I don't

intend to be. You're *lost*. All of you. I'm not lost. I'm not one of you.

(JESSICA goes. The three stand there for a long moment of silence.)

JEN. We're lost?

ELLY. She's right. We are lost.

GAYLE. Yeah. I guess we are. *(Beat.)* But at least--we know it.

ELLY. And at least we have sense of humor about it, geez—

JEN. No shit. *We're* lost? She's going to fucking Jeffrey's—

ELLY. She rejected *us* for Jeffrey? What kind of fucked up is that?

GAYLE. Well, you did pull a knife on her.

ELLY. I apologized!

JEN. Hey, you think this means we'll get the house?

GAYLE. Jen!

JEN. What? She thinks we're lost, she's not one of us; it sounds to me like we're gonna get the house.

ELLY. Sounds that way to me.

JEN. Yes! I think that's excellent.

(ELLY and JEN give each other the high five.)

GAYLE. We're not getting the house! Or, maybe you are. But I'm moving out.

JEN. You are?

GAYLE. Yes. I am.

ELLY. Gayle—

GAYLE. We'll talk about it on the way to the police station.

JEN. The police station? Why are we going to the police station.

ELLY. You got beat up!

JEN. Oh, yeah. But you know, I'm not kidding, you guys. We can't go to the cops because they'll arrest the wrong person. Richardson looks worse than I do.

GAYLE. He does?

JEN. I pounded him. Well, he won the fight. But he looks *bad*.

ELLY. Good. I'm glad you punished that jerk. We're still going to the police.

JEN. Elly—

ELLY. Jen, it's just that if he got violent once, he can get violent again, and— *(Beat.)* Shit.

JEN. It's okay, Elly.

ELLY. No, it's not. I mean violence is not good. It's not just a mistake, you know? *(Beat.)* I am a bad person, aren't I?

GAYLE. No, you're not a bad person. But if you ever pull a knife on me, I'll murder you.

ELLY. Fair enough.

GAYLE. *(Beat.)* But for now we are going to take this girl to the hospital, and I don't want anymore arguments about it. I have no intention of ever going through a day like this again, so starting tonight, we are going to fucking deal. We're going to the hospital, I'll check you in myself and we can fill out the police report from there.

(They ALL stand, gathering jackets, shoes and keys.)

ELLY. If you move, can we come with you?

GAYLE. We'll talk about it on the way to the hospital.

JEN. Real rent, huh? You think we're capable of real rent?

GAYLE. I think we're capable of anything.

JEN. Hey, can we stop for doughnuts? What? If you guys are going to take care of me, then do it right.

ELLY. Hey, is your new boyfriend going to be there?

JEN. What boyfriend? Where?

GAYLE. Elly—

ELLY. *(To JEN.)* Gayle's new boyfriend works at the hospital.

GAYLE. He's not—

ELLY. He's a shrink. His name is Phil. Keep your eyes open.

GAYLE. You have the biggest mouth!

ELLY. Big mouth? Me?

GAYLE. You're not moving in with me.

ELLY. Come on...

(The door slams as they leave.)

BLACKOUT

END OF PLAY

PROPERTY LIST

Lots of Ice, for about 6 or 7 galsses - plastic
4 Tumblers or large scotch glasses
1 Juice/Water Glass
2 Bottles of Scotch with tops
Sunday Boston Newspaper w/comic section
Pack of Marlboro lights
Lighter / Ashtray
Telephone
Stereo with cassette deck, volume knob. on/off buttons
Cassette tapes
Ouija board, cursor and the box it comes in
1 plate
3 mugs/coffee cups
5 Magazines
Magazine w/crossword - Pencil
Cheeseboard
Sharp knife for cheesboard
Matching dull knife for fight at end of show
2 key rings with keys
Books
Bottle of aspirin
Detachable lampshade
Carafe for coffee
4 cushions wicker chairs
2 throw pillows for couch
Lamp
3 pair of sunglasses
Dishcloth
Purse
Napkin
Bottle of ginger ale

PERISHABLES:
Scotch
Oatmeal cookies
Water
Herbal cigarettes / Lighter
Apple
1/4 toasted English muffin
Box of Cheerios

FURNITURE:
Thin table w/drawer for telephone
2 wicker chairs--*one chair with a hole poked through it, we think the hole is through the seat of the chair, but it's not clearly stated in the script and the chair is carried offstage.*
Wicker couch
Wicker table
Couch
Easy chair
Small table for lamp
Bookcase--*referred to in script - "I need my keys. I left them on the bookcase."*
Coffee table
Hassock
Solid door
Screen door
Porch railing (sawhorses)
Platform w/bar - 2 bar stools

PROPS ENTRANCES AND EXITS

PRESET: On Stage
FURNITURE: On Porch
2 wicker chairs, SR one has hole on left arm

wicker couch
wicker table
5 ft. bench

On Platform:
couch
easy chair
hassock
coffee table
lamp table
table upstage of couch
platform w/bar
2 bar stools
bookcase

HAND PROPS:
On Porch:
2 pillows on wicker couch
1 pillow on the other 2 wicker chairs
door stop by screen door
On Wicker Table:
big glass--half full, poured from bottle
3 ice cubes in glass
bottle of scotch with top

On Platform:
both doors closed

On Bookcase:
stereo
2 cassette tapes
books
Gayle's keys

On Upstage Table:
telephone
2 magazines--that stay there throughout the show
3 pair sunglasses
In drawer--magazine w/crossword & pencil

On Coffee Table:
3 magazines, scattered--that stay there throughout the show.

On Couch:
5 sections Boston Sunday paper, including comics
2 throw pillows, one either end

On Lamp Table:
lampshade on lamp

On Kitchen Props Table:
tumbler with OJ
half eaten toasted English muffin
tumbler with 2 ice cubes
ashtray
pack of cigarettes
lighter
carafe of coffee
bottle of ginger ale
bottle of aspirin
discloth
2 ice cubes
tumbler w/water
ouija board
box for board
cursor

On Bedroom Props Table:
plate of oatmeal cookies
cheeseboard
apple
sharp knife
dull knife
full bottle of scotch
key ring
Jessica's purse
3 coffee mugs

Act I. Sc. 1:

Gayle's Entrance onto Porch (p.7)

tumbler with OJ
half eaten English muffin
shoes--stay at door until the end of show

Jen's Entrance onto Porch (p. 11)

newspaper

Elly's re-entrance onto porch (p.13)

pack of cigarettes w/cellophane?
lighter
tumbler with 2 ice cubes
ashtray

END OF ACT I, SC. 1 SET UP:

On Porch:

On Floor:

a section of paper between SR wicker chair and couch
section of paper between SR wicker chair and table cushion
        SR side couch DAC

On Bench:

Gayle holding her tumbler w/1 cubes
Jen holding Elly's glass and the bottle

On Wicker Table:

tumbler w/2 ice cubes
lighter
English muffin
napkin
ashtray
cigarettes

On SL Wicker Chair:

cushion from SR end couch

On Platform:

no change

SET UP ACT I, SC. 2;

On Porch:

On Floor:

a section of paper between SR wicker chair and couch
a section of paper between SR wicker chair and table
SR cushion of couch DSC

On Wicker Table:

English muffin & napkin

On Platform:

Stereo opens
Gayle holding Scotch bottle
All three wearing shades
Elly's coat hangs on hook and stays there through end of show

<u>On Coffee Table:</u>

a glass, with ice
2 tumblers, with ice
cigarettes
lighter
ashtray
box of cereal

<u>On Floor:</u>

SL of couch 1 section of newspaper

<u>ACT I, SC. 2;</u>
<u>Elly Enters From Bedroom (p. 38)</u>
full bottle of Scotch

<u>SET UP END OF ACT I, SC.2</u>
<u>On Porch:</u>

same as beginning of Act I, Sc. 1

<u>On Platform:</u>
<u>On Lamp Table:</u>

Elly's glass w/ice

<u>On Floor:</u>

telephone SL of coffee table
lampshade US of lamp table
newspaper SL of couch
box of cereal SL of coffee table

<u>On Coffee Table:</u>

2 bottles of Scotch
2 tumblers w/ice
cigarettes

106

lighter
ashtray

On Bar:
Gayle's shades

On US Table:
Jen's shades
Elly's shades

SET UP ACT I, SC.3:
On Porch:
same as Act I, Sc. 2

On Platform:
add butts to ashtray
phone back on US table
hassock moves DS of easy chair
Ouija board and cursor on hassock
stereo stays open

On Coffee Table:
3 coffee mugs
knife
ashtray
lighter
cheeseboard
apple
plate w/cookies
2 bottles of scotch
2 tumblers, ice

On Floor:
lampshade US of lamptable
a section of newspaper SL of couch
box of ouija DSC in hassock's place
box of cereal SL CT

On Lamptable:
Elly's glass, ice

In Elly's Hand:
crossword puzzle & pencil

ACT I, Sc. 3:
Jen Enters From Kitchen (p. 49)
carafe of coffee

Gayle Enters From Kitchen (p. 53)
aspirin
bottle of ginger ale

Jessica Enters From Front of House (p. 56)
purse
keys
sweater

SET UP END OF ACT I, SC. 3:
On Porch:
three sections of paper:
          1 on floor SL of SR wicker chair
          1 on floor SR of SR wicker chair
On Platform:
stero stays open
Jessica holding purse, keys & sweater

On Couch:
_____
ouija board in box
section of paper on SL cushion

On Lamp Table:
_____
Elly's glass
2 coffee mugs

On Floor:
_____
section paper SL of couch
lampshade US of lamp table
box of cereal SL of CT
pencil

On US Table:
_____
bottle of ginger ale
aspirin
Jen's shades

On Bar:
_____
Gayle's shades

On Coffee Table:
_____
coffee mug
2 tumblers
cheeseboard w/fruit
knife
ashtray
lighter
cigarettes
carafe coffee
2 bottles of Scotch
plate w/cookies

Intermission:
nothing moves

SET UP ACT II, Sc. 1:
same as end Act I, Sc. 3

ACT II, Sc. 1:
Jessica Exits Through House (p. 71)
wicker chair w/hole

Elly Exits to Kitchen (p. 75)
2 tumblers
a mug

SET UP END OF ACT II, SC. 1:
On Porch:
SR wicker chair offstage
SR cushion couch is back on couch

SET UP END OF ACT II, SC. 1:
On Porch:
SR wicker chair offstage
SR cushion couch is back on couch

On Platform:
hassock DSC
sterio stays open
ouija board, box, cursor US of bookcase
lampshade is back on lamp

On Coffee Table:
cheesboard
fruit

knife
2 bottles of Scotch
ashtray
cigarettes
lighter

On Bookcase:

purse
keys
sweater

On Bar:

Gayle's shades

On Stool:

newspaper

On US Table:

2 mugs
plate of cookies
napkin & muffin
carafe
ashtray
aspirin
cigarettes
lighter
bottle of ginger ale
Jen's shades
Elly's shades
box of cereal
In drawer: magazine w/ crossword & pencil

111

SET UP ACT II, SC. 2:

On Porch:

the same as end of Act II, Sc. 1

On Platform:

hassock is DSC

lmapshade is on lamp

On Lamp Table:

new bottle of Scotch

Elly's glass w/ice & Scotch

On Coffee Table:

cheeseboard - on SR end

fruit

dull knife - set diagonally, handle facing US S1 corner of board

On Bookcase:

keys - 2 sets

On US Table:

3 pair shades

ACT II, SC. 2:

Elly Enters From Kitchen (p. 85)

dishcloth

2 ice cubes

Gayle Enters From Kitchen (p. 86)

aspirin

glass w/water

OTHER TITLES AVAILABLE FROM SAMUEL FRENCH

CAPTIVE
Jan Buttram

Comedy / 2m, 1f / Interior

A hilarious take on a father/daughter relationship, this off beat comedy combines foreign intrigue with down home philosophy. Sally Pound flees a bad marriage in New York and arrives at her parent's home in Texas hoping to borrow money from her brother to pay a debt to gangsters incurred by her husband. Her elderly parents are supposed to be vacationing in Israel, but she is greeted with a shotgun aimed by her irascible father who has been left home because of a minor car accident and is not at all happy to see her. When a news report indicates that Sally's mother may have been taken captive in the Middle East, Sally's hard-nosed brother insists that she keep father home until they receive definite word, and only then will he loan Sally the money. Sally fails to keep father in the dark, and he plans a rescue while she finds she is increasingly unable to skirt the painful truths of her life. The ornery father and his loveable but slightly-dysfunctional daughter come to a meeting of hearts and minds and solve both their problems.

OTHER TITLES AVAILABLE FROM SAMUEL FRENCH

TAKE HER, SHE'S MINE
Phoebe and Henry Ephron

Comedy / 11m, 6f / Various Sets

Art Carney and Phyllis Thaxter played the Broadway roles of parents of two typical American girls enroute to college. The story is based on the wild and wooly experiences the authors had with their daughters, Nora Ephron and Delia Ephron, themselves now well known writers. The phases of a girl's life are cause for enjoyment except to fearful fathers. Through the first two years, the authors tell us, college girls are frightfully sophisticated about all departments of human life. Then they pass into the "liberal" period of causes and humanitarianism, and some into the intellectual lethargy of beatniksville. Finally, they start to think seriously of their lives as grown ups. It's an experience in growing up, as much for the parents as for the girls.

"A warming comedy. A delightful play about parents vs kids. It's loaded with laughs. It's going to be a smash hit."
– *New York Mirror*

SAMUEL FRENCH STAFF

Nate Collins
President

Ken Dingledine
Director of Operations,
Vice President

Bruce Lazarus
Executive Director,
General Counsel

Rita Maté
Director of Finance

ACCOUNTING

Lori Thimsen | Director of Licensing Compliance
Nehal Kumar | Senior Accounting Associate
Charles Graytok | Accounting and Finance Manager
Glenn Halcomb | Royalty Administration
Jessica Zheng | Accounts Receivable
Andy Lian | Accounts Payable
Charlie Sou | Accounting Associate
Joann Mannello | Orders Administrator

BUSINESS AFFAIRS

Caitlin Bartow | Assistant to the Executive Director

CORPORATE COMMUNICATIONS

Abbie Van Nostrand | Director of Corporate
Communications

CUSTOMER SERVICE AND LICENSING

Laura Lindson | Licensing Services Manager
Kim Rogers | Theatrical Specialist
Matthew Akers | Theatrical Specialist
Ashley Byrne | Theatrical Specialist
Jennifer Carter | Theatrical Specialist
Annette Storckman | Theatrical Specialist
Julia Izumi | Theatrical Specialist
Sarah Weber | Theatrical Specialist
Nicholas Dawson | Theatrical Specialist
David Kimple | Theatrical Specialist
Ryan McLeod | Theatrical Specialist
Carly Erickson | Theatrical Specialist

EDITORIAL

Amy Rose Marsh | Literary Manager
Ben Coleman | Literary Associate

MARKETING

Ryan Pointer | Marketing Manager
Courtney Kochuba | Marketing Associate
Chris Kam | Marketing Associate

PUBLICATIONS AND PRODUCT DEVELOPMENT

David Geer | Publications Manager
Tyler Mullen | Publications Associate
Emily Sorensen | Publications Associate
Derek P. Hassler | Musical Products Coordinator
Zachary Orts | Musical Materials Coordinator

OPERATIONS

Casey McLain | Operations Supervisor
Elizabeth Minski | Office Coordinator, Reception
Coryn Carson | Office Coordinator, Reception

SAMUEL FRENCH BOOKSHOP (LOS ANGELES)

Joyce Mehess | Bookstore Manager
Cory DeLair | Bookstore Buyer
Kristen Springer | Customer Service Manager
Tim Coultas | Bookstore Associate
Bryan Jansyn | Bookstore Associate
Alfred Contreras | Shipping & Receiving

LONDON OFFICE

Anne-Marie Ashman | Accounts Assistant
Felicity Barks | Rights & Contracts Associate
Steve Blacker | Bookshop Associate
David Bray | Customer Services Associate
Robert Cooke | Assistant Buyer
Stephanie Dawson | Amateur Licensing Associate
Simon Ellison | Retail Sales Manager
Robert Hamilton | Amateur Licensing Associate
Peter Langdon | Marketing Manager
Louise Mappley | Amateur Licensing Associate
James Nicolau | Despatch Associate
Emma Anacootee-Parmar | Production/Editorial
Controller
Martin Phillips | Librarian
Panos Panayi | Company Accountant
Zubayed Rahman | Despatch Associate
Steve Sanderson | Royalty Administration Supervisor
Douglas Schatz | Acting Executive Director
Roger Sheppard | I.T. Manager
Debbie Simmons | Licensing Sales Team Leader
Peter Smith | Amateur Licensing Associate
Garry Spratley | Customer Service Manager
David Webster | UK Operations Director
Sarah Wolf | Rights Director